This book is dedicated to Dena Hartman

All characters in this book are fictitious, and any resemblance to actual persons living or dead is purely coincidental.

Special thanks to Janet Stout & Eric Schweska.

Al Hartman
2016

Spitfire Mustang

After the Civil War, whatever was so civil about it, 650,000 men died, a lot of Southerners and ex Union Soldiers that served in the Western Theater went home, packed up, and moved their families west. During the war when a Confederate soldier was captured he was offered a job in the Union Army to fight in the west rather than go to a prison camp. A lot of Confederates took that offer rather than the alternative.

The Union Army thought by sending the Confederates west, they would not try to escape, being so far from home. It mostly worked out very well as most of the fighting was with Indians since most tribes joined allegiance to the Southern cause. There were some Grey versus Blue battles which caused uneasy feeling with the boys from the south as it made them feel like traitors.

The Confederate soldiers returned to a devastated and financially ruined Southland. Cities, towns and farms were destroyed and burned to ruins and had to make a new start. The memory of all that vast open beautiful country was on their minds beckoning them to return.

A lot of Union soldiers, and the men from the South, had never seen territory such as it was in the west. So open and vast. Seeming like it never ended. Mountains, plains, buttes, mesas and bluffs with buffalo, deer, elk and antelope. Such a magnificent country it was to behold. Many soldiers yearned to return and start a new life.

Spitfire Mustang

Chapter One June 1876

Alan Holt was returning to Texas after helping John Witt, his sons, and some cowpokes drive a herd of cattle from Laramie Plains, Wyoming, to the rail yard in Hays City, Kansas. It was a drive through the plains of Nebraska and into the heart of central Kansas. They encountered several bands of Indians, but only had trouble twice with a couple of bands trying to steal some of their cattle. Both times they managed to drive them off without anyone wounded or killed from the Witt's crew. One band they met along the drive had older men, women and children and they looked as they were starving. Most drives would have ignored them, but John Witt felt sorry for the weary braves, women and children and he gave them a nice fat steer to feed them. The small band really appreciated his kindness and told him they would ask the Great Chief in the sky to always look over him, his family, his men and their family's. Evidently they did, because as the years went on the Great Chief did look over the Witt's

John Witt met Alan in a bar in Minersville, Wyoming. Alan was looking for work and John Witt heard Alan say to the bartender he knew the best trail to Hays City, Kansas. After talking to Alan, John determined Alan knew what he was talking about and hired him to head the drive as trail boss.

It took nearly six weeks to make the drive and after the cattle were sold Alan was paid five hundred dollars, a very good payday for him or anyone in these times. He was going to save as much of that money he could, and build up enough to buy a place of his own one day. That was his dream, to have a spread to call his own and raise a family. He stayed a couple of days in Hays City to rest up and then started heading to Texas as it was late May and coming into calving season and it wouldn't be too hard to find work there right now, as cattleman were needed to round up the cattle and brand the newly dropped calves.

He headed south and knew he had to be on alert and be very careful as he would be riding alone through Indian Territory. That's what Oklahoma was known as at this time. There was no shortage of different tribes to watch for. There were bands of Cherokees, Choctaw, Comanche's and Kiowa's. Not to mention the Apaches in and around Texas. Most were tolerant of white men but not all were so eager to be friendly. Alan knew a lot about them all as he worked with the Army as a scout for several years. Lately the Sioux and the Cheyenne were gathering in large numbers and causing trouble, that worried him.

What worried Alan the most was the Kiowa. He figured they killed more white people and Indians than all the others tribes put together. They were country wise and vicious brutal killers. And they didn't treat their Indian neighbors much better, always warring with other tribes. Alan tried to keep off the main trails as much as he could, and ride in the tree lines when it was possible. When he camped he looked for a low spot with cover to hide him and his horse. He made just enough fire to cook on and used wood that would give off heat but not much smoke.

He put on just enough wood to keep the fire going at night, for embers in the morning.

He had found a nice area with a stream nearby to camp. He tethered his Grulla stallion, who he called Buddy, in a grassy rich area for the night and made some coffee and bacon on bread for dinner. After eating he rolled a smoke and relaxed watching the moon rise. He made his bed roll under a rock overhang. He finished his smoke and dozed off to sleep. The coyotes were howling and he could hear an owl calling for a mate from time to time. Not sure how long he had been asleep, he heard Buddy murmur. Buddy could smell an Indian in a ninety mile an hour wind storm, and Buddy didn't like Indians at all. One night when they were camping, Buddy kicked a brave knocking him to the ground as he was trying to steal him. Then Buddy stomped him to death. He just didn't like Indians.

Alan awoke and all was quiet and deathly still. He knew Buddy was alerting him and knew trouble might be in the works. He eased to a dark spot between two large rocks with a ledge over them and pulled out his Colt and leaned his rifle beside him. Buddy murmured again. Alan could make his horse out in the darkness but wasn't worried about anyone stealing him. That was very unlikely. He sat there in the dark hollow and heard and saw nothing. Then he felt sand hit his hat from above. "He's above and behind me looking down," He thought to himself. Alan eased his rifle to the front of his chest and waited careful not to make any noise. Sand came down on his hat again. Alan took his rifle and pointed it up and back very carefully and pulled the trigger. He heard a smack and an Indian brave fell almost in his lap with a thud. He then heard a noise in front of him and saw two shapes rushing toward his concealed spot. He pointed his Colt and fired three quick shots which found their mark and the two braves fell. Alan sat and waited on the alert. After deciding there were no more to contend with he got up. The Indian that fell beside him was shot low in the forehead. He then went to check the other two. One took a hit dead center in the chest and the other was hit in the mid section twice, both dead! He walked over to Buddy and rubbed his nose.

"Thanks Buddy boy," he said, "You saved the day ole boy. I owe ya once again pal." He dragged the braves next to where he had slept and buried them the best he could then piled some rocks over them. He very cautiously walked around checking against any more surprises. He found two of the Indian ponies one of which was a pretty Pinto mare. He walked right up to her and took her lead with no problem. The other one spooked off. Alan walked back to his camp. He was thinking she had been a white mans horse before the Indians got her as most Indian ponies shied away from a white man.

"Got ya a present Buddy boy," he said, and walked up to Buddy. Buddy sniffed her up and down and she acted like she didn't notice him with her ears laid back. Acting just like a lady does playing hard to get and acting disinterested.

Allan made some coffee but didn't want to dally too long in case those Indian ponies he had scattered got back to their camp empty. Then the band would be hunting him. He didn't identify what tribe they were from, maybe a band of mixed renegades. He drank his coffee and covered the remains of the fire, and then saddled up Buddy and got the Pinto mare to follow. She had to have been a stolen ranch horse as she followed right behind, he was thinking. Riding the tree lines as much as he could to keep from being seen, he would stop and check his back trail here and there to make sure he wasn't being followed. Alan was not sure if he had been seen yesterday, or those braves just happened to chance up on his camp smelling the smoke from his fire. He didn't know, but it kept him alert and watchful.

Chapter Two

Late in the afternoon he saw the city of Dodge in the distance. Dodge was a big city that had more saloons than churches or stores. It was a big cattleman's town.
Alan stopped Buddy near a pool of water and let the stallion and the mare drink. While the Grulla and the Pinto were drinking Alan pulled the five hundred dollars cash from his pocket and put most of it in his right boot in a empty tobacco sack. He didn't want to be flashing a large sum of money while in Dodge as that could be risky. Dodge City was always a tough town but with calving season in, there would be a lot more cowboys, gamblers, thieves, and some just outright undesirables in town. Robbery was the number one crime next to murder from gun fights. Charles Bassett was the sheriff and he had his hands full keeping the peace, coupled with the problem that some of the deputies were outright outlaws themselves. He did have in his favor, Wyatt Earp and Bat Masterson as undersheriff's working for him. Not many men wanted a job that paid forty to sixty dollars a month to be shot at.
Alan rode into town and it was booming with excitement. The streets were full of cowpokes, drifters, miners and drunks. Honky-tonk music was coming from the saloons and an occasional shot was fired as the drunken cowhands were having a good time and it wasn't even dark yet. Alan saw a livery stable and rode to it.
"Howdy partner." A short stocky man hollered at him. "Can a be of any help to ya?"

"I'd like to put my horses in your corral while I get something to eat," Alan answered, "And I'd like to take a nap in your loft for an hour or so before moving on."
"We got a hotel's here." The stocky man answered.
"Don't want to stay in town. I'd like to get moving on toward Texas to find some work."
"Plenty of ranches hiring around here me boy. Don't gotta' go all the way to Texas."
"Got my mind set on Texas." Alan replied. "Lookin' for work and land to settle. That's been on my mind for a while."
"Suit yourself partner, four bits an' feed the horses too!"
Alan paid the man a silver dollar and took the saddle off Buddy and placed on a saddle rack. There was a water pump beside the building and Alan washed his face, hands and washed out his hair. He thanked the hostler and walked across the street. There was a barber pole next to the Longhorn Saloon and that looked good to Alan as he did need a shave. He walked in and the barber an elderly man with graying hair was in the chair reading the Dodge City Times.
"Howdy friend." The barber said. "Can I help ya?"
"I'd like a shave if you got time sir."
"Got all the time in the world friend. Just a shave young man? I can throw in a hair trim for extra two bits."
"Just a shave will do me sir."
"Names Rob, Rob Dunn young fella. What's yours?"
"Alan Holt."
"Been here before Alan?"

“It’s been a while since I’ve been in Dodge. Passed through Dodge a couple times. Is it any better here than it was a couple of years ago?”
“Sheriff Charlie Bassett’s doing a decent job of holding down trouble. Don’t envy his job a bit. James “Dog” Kelly is the new Mayor an he’s standing behind Bassett all the way, he is.”
Rob the barber and Alan talked about old times, Earp, Masterson, and other lawmen. Then indians, cattlemen, and a man by the name of Bell who is saying you can talk to a person over a wire now. Just how are you going to do that, they discussed. The hot towels and shave felt real good. He paid Rob for the shave combed his hair and asked about a good place to get a meal.
“Long Branch Saloon has got good meals and reasonable too!” The barber replied.
“Thanks, I’ll give it a try.” Alan said, and walked outside.
The town was full of cowboys, miners, and men getting supplies coming and going. He walked into the Long Branch and went to the bar. It was crowded elbow to elbow. The gaming tables were doing a good business. The saloon was quite crowded. At one table he saw Bat Masterson with his derby hat playing cards.
Note;
(The movies and TV shows portray Masterson with a cane. The fact was he was shot in the hip in a gun fight and used a cane for a while until he healed. He didn’t use a cane until later in life when working for the New York City Police Department, early nineteenth century.)

Alan found a spot to stand at the bar, and the bartender walked down to him.
"What can I get ya fella?" He asked.
"I'll take a shot of rye and would like to get a meal if I can." Alan answered.
"We can take care of that." The bartender said as he poured Alan a shot. "Find yer' self a table an' I'll get ya a waitress to take yer order."
There wasn't an empty table in the house. He saw a table with two men talking and walked over to them.
"Would you men mind if I sat here to eat my meal?"
"Not a'tall, have a seat fella. We're just killing time"
Alan pulled out a chair and sat down. "Thanks," he said, and took a sip of his drink. One of the men pushed a bottle toward him and told Alan to help himself. Alan nodded in reply. A young lady came to the table.
"Hi, my name's Bryanna Cayson. I'll be taking your order. What can I get you?"
Alan asked for a steak and a baked potato.
"Want gravy on that?" Bryanna asked.
"Just on the potato." Alan answered. "An' I want my steak on the rare side if I can."
"Hot rolls and butter comes with that too!" She told him.
"Good, hot rolls will be a treat."
Bryanna wrote it down on a slip of paper and told him it would be ready soon and walked away.
"You passin' through?" One of the men asked.
"Yes, going on to Texas. Going to try an' find some work there on a cattle ranch."

“Plenty of work here young man. No need to go all the way to Texas.”

“Got my mind set on Texas. Hope to find some land an’ make my own spread in time.”

“I wish ya luck my boy.” The older man of the two said. “Better be on the look out though as yer passin’ through pretty bad Indian Territory an’ some of ‘em ain’t too friendly now- a- days.”

“I’ve already found that out last night. I got ambushed by three braves. Lucky my horse warned me an I got them before they got me.”

“Damn good horse, fella.”

“Yea he hates indians.” Alan told him.

Bryanna brought Alan’s meal and told him to let her know if he needed anything more. Alan talked with the men as he ate his meal. One of the men asked if he would sell his horse.

“No I’m gonna’ keep that Stallion, he’s a good ride and a smart horse. Don’t have to worry about anyone ridin’ off with him either.” Alan then told them about Buddy killing an indian that tried to steel him once. They were impressed. Wyatt Earp walked into the saloon and that caught everyone’s attention. Wyatt walked to the table that Bat was sitting at and had a word with him and Bat excused himself from the card game and they both walked out.

“Must ‘a be sometin’ going on,” one of the men said, “They looked mighty serious. Always something goin’ on here in Dodge,” the other man replied, “every day for sure. Well see ya around cowboy, gotta’ go, take care an’ watch yer back.”

The two men got up walked to the bar paid their tab and walked out of the saloon waving at Alan as they went by. Alan finished his meal, paid Bryanna, and went outside. It was getting toward sundown. Alan went back to the livery stable and the hostler told him it was OK to use the loft.
"Make yer self cozy, my boy, just don't smoke up there. Don't wanta' set the barn afire."
"I smoke outside, fella' seen many a barn burn because of carelessness. I don't wanta' do that"
Alan rolled a smoke and went to check on Buddy and the Pinto mare. Buddy nuzzled him and murmured a little. Alan carefully mashed his smoke into the dirt went into the barn and climbed into the loft, rolled out his blanket and laid down to relax. It felt good to get some rest. He laid there listening to the town noise. Horses coming and going, saloon pianos playing and a gun shot here and there. "It's hard to go to sleep with all this noise," he thought to himself. Although it felt good to lay and relax, sleep was hard to come by with all this noise out side for a man that's spent so much time in the wilderness listening for danger signals.
He was just about to doze off when he heard some rustling down on the barn floor. Then someone was climbing up the ladder to the loft. Alan grabbed his Colt and pointed it at opening of the loft. He could see a head pop up over the edge but couldn't make out who it was. He cocked his pistol with his finger on the trigger so not to make a click to warn the intruder.
"You up here?" A female voice asked.
" Who's asking and who's the you your looking for?"

“I served you a meal tonight at the Long Branch. I’m Bryanna, Bryanna Cayson.”

“What can I do for you, Bryanna?”

“I want to sleep with you tonight, please.”

Alan rolled his eyes and shook his head. “I don’t think that would be appropriate, missy, you being a youngin’, now why don’t you go back an’ dry behind your ears.”

“I ain’t no youngin’, I’m a woman.”

“How old are you?”

“I’m sixteen, well next week that is.”

“You better get back before your mom gets here an tries to blame for something I had no mind of doin’.”

“Look I’ll do anything you ask mister cause I need your help and I have no one to turn too.”

“What do you mean? Where’s your family?”

“I lived with my grandparents before I was brought here. They don’t know where I am and I couldn’t contact them because no one would take a message to them. My grandparents probably thinks I’m dead or been captured by Indians.”

“O K, climb up here an’ tell me what’s going on.”

Bryanna climbed up and over to where Alan was sitting. She told him she went for a ride a couple of months ago on her horse and a rattlesnake spooked her horse and he threw her off. She tried to catch him but he kept running away from her. When it got dark and she couldn’t see the horse anymore she climbed up on a pile of rocks and spent a very cold night. When she woke in the morning she was shivering from the cold until the sun got higher. After chasing the horse she became confused and didn’t know which way was home and there was no sign of the horse. She had no water or a hat for her head and the sun beat down on her. She told him there were snakes, scorpions and lizards of all kinds everywhere. Finally late in the afternoon she saw four riders off in the distance. She waved and hollered and whistled at then to get their attention. They saw her and rode to her. She said a big rough looking man sat on his horse with a grin on his face and asked her how she got where she was. Bryanna said she explained to him what had happened and asked if he would help her. The man said he would, and took her to a cabin not far from Dodge City and let her clean up and fed her some bacon and bread. Bryanna asked when could he return her home and told her to get some rest and he would take her in the morning. She told Alan that he kept looking at her in a way that he was looking through her clothes. She felt uneasy.

"So what happened then?" Alan asked. "Did he try to take you home?"

"No he didn't. When I got out of bed he put me on his horse and he took me here into Dodge and to the Long Branch Saloon."

"To get you help?"

"No, to put me to work! When I resisted he took me into a room on the side and beat the hell out of me and he never hit my face so it would show. He told me that if I told anyone or went to the law he would drag me behind his horse until I was dead."

"OK, let me take you to the sheriff."

"It wont do any good, Bryanna told Alan, "He and the sheriff are buddies. His name is Will Markus and he showed me papers he had gotten made up showing him as my legal guardian." Alan just shook his head.
Suddenly a voice rang out. "Bryanna, you up there?"
Alan told her to be quiet and said. "There's no Bryanna up here, look elsewhere."
"I know she's there," the man said, "Followed her tracks to this here latter. Now send her down."
"Ain't no one comin' down." Alan replied.
"OK then, I'll drag ya' down."
Two shots rang out and they ripped through the barn loft floor sending splinters through the air. Suddenly a voice shouted, "Drop it mister, drop it now or I'll make ya' look like a sieve." It sounded like the man who owned the stable.
The man on the ground floor must have turned and pointed his pistol at the barn owner as the blast from a double barreled shotgun roared.
"Y'all OK up there?" The man asked. "Don't worry about him. He's not gonna' bother you."
"Thanks fella'," Alan replied. "Thanks a bunch. Come on Bryanna, I'll take ya' home."
Alan and Bryanna climbed down the ladder. The dead man on the barn floor was Will Markus.
"Dint' wanta' see you hurt an' dint' want more holes in my loft either." The stocky stable owner told Alan. "This here scum traded young girls for favors an' money. Kept 'em as slaves he did."

“He told me he was gonna’ have me sleepin’ with cowboys starting next week.” Byanna said. “Glad he’s dead, now I can go home.”

Chapter Three

Alan paid the stable owner his fare for keeping the horses, saddled Buddy and put Bryanna on the pinto mare.

"Where we gotta' go to get you home?" Alan asked.

"Near Montezuma," Bryanna told him, "Just a little north. Not sure how to get there from here though."

The livery man told Alan, "It's bout forty miles southwest a here, just follow the wagon tracks, an' be keeping yer eyes open cause injuns done be riled up. Sometin's stirring fer sure."

"I found that out coming here," Alan replied, "I was attacked the night before I came in to Dodge by three Indians dressed in war paint."

"Wanta' stay till morning young man?"

"No I want to get a head start an' traveling in the dark will keep us hidden some what."

"OK young fella, you be careful."

Alan thanked him again and headed out of town with Bryanna riding behind him. They rode all night stopping only once to take a private break and water the horses at a stream near the road. Once and a while Alan could see fires from travelers camping, or in was Indians so he kept clear of them just in case.

It was a clear night and jack rabbits were running from them and a coyote would cry out from time to time.. Bryanna didn't have a jacket so Alan gave her his blanket to pull over her shoulders to relieve the chill of the night. As the sun started to rise Alan stopped near a stream and started to make some coffee. He used good dried hard wood as not to make any smoke that would signal anyone of their presents. He cut some bacon chunks and cooked them on sticks over the fire to give them something to put in their stomachs. He was very tired and needed some rest but the coffee and bacon helped him to refresh some what. After eating they kept heading southwest, keeping in the brush or as close to what few areas of sparse tree lines as much as possible. About noon time Bryanna said, "See that rock formation that looks like a fist with a finger pointing to the sky? Grandpa calls that Indian finger rock. Our farm is about two miles past that."

"Great," Alan answered, "Your almost home an' we didn't run into any trouble, thankfully!"

They rode on and the farm came into sight. When they got to the gate Alan saw a stocky heavy man plowing rows with a mule. The man waved, most likely not knowing who they were, just being friendly. They rode up to the house and a heavy set woman came out of the front door. She stood there for a moment and her eyes went big and her mouth dropped open.

"My good heavens," the lady said, "Bryanna your alive."

"Yes grandma, this man saved me and my freedom."

"Well may the good Lord bless him." She said, then ran over and gave Bryanna and big hug and kissed her cheek. She turned to Alan standing there holding Buddy. "I'm Leslie Henderson, young man, thank you so much for bringing her home. We thought she may have been killed or captured."

"Well she was captured, but not by Indians, ma'am. I'm Alan Holt. I'll let her tell you about it."

“Come in and have some coffee. Do you want something to eat? I can fix something up quickly.”
“That would be nice ma’am, I could go for both.”
They went into the house and sat at a table. Mrs. Henderson kept hugging Bryanna. She was overjoyed. The stocky, heavy man came into the house and shouted Brianna’s name and he picked her up off the floor and spun her around. It was Paul Henderson, Leslie’s husband.
“I can’t believe my eyes. We thought you were a goner for sure.” He said. “Never heard a word from anyone. We went on a search for you for days but found no tracks or signs of you after we found your horse.”
“He was a stinky. Wouldn’t let me catch him Grandpa, he just ran off an’ left me.”
They sat at the table and Bryanna told them of her capture and what she had gone through under the hand of Will Markus.
“I’m gonna’ ride to Dodge an’ kill him.” Paul told them.
“No need for that Mr. Henderson,” Alan replied, “The stable owner took care of that for you and it saved us a lot of trouble too.”
Mrs. Henderson made some hot coffee, bacon and hot cakes with butter and honey. Alan was starved and he ate several. After eating he asked, “Sir, do you mind if I make a bed in your barn to get some rest?”
“I won’t hear of that young man,” Leslie told him, “You freshen up and we have an extra bed in the side room for you to use. You rest all you want.”
“Thanks ma’am that would by wonderful.” She handed Alan a wash rag, soap and a towel and showed him where

the pump house was. It felt good to wash up and he returned to the house. Paul showed him to the bedroom. Alan kicked off his boots, dropped his pants, pulled off his shirt, and laid down on the bed. He fell asleep immediately.

When Alan awoke the sun was up. "Boy did I sleep." He thought to himself. He went to the wash house with the towel rapped him carrying his cloths. After freshening up he went back to the house and Mrs. Henderson was making bacon, biscuits and eggs.

"Have some breakfast Alan." She told him. "You don't know how much we appreciate all you did to bring her home. We don't know how to thank you enough."

"Glad I could help her ma'am. She had gotten into a fix for sure, an' was in for some bad times and maybe an' early death."

"We really thank you Alan. Now fill yourself up, there's plenty more here if you want it."

Alan ate a big helping. It felt good to relax and enjoy a home cooked meal. He had caught up on his rest and felt great. Alan thanked the Henderson for their hospitality and told them that he had to move on for Texas.

"You come back an' see us." Paul said and shook Alan's hand. Bryanna thanked Alan and she and Mrs. Henderson each gave him big hugs.

Alan tipped his hat and thanked them again and went out to saddle up Buddy and get the pinto mare. As he mounted up, Bryanna was standing near.

"I'll never forget you Alan,….never will." They waved at each other; Alan turned and rode down the lane through the gate.

Chapter Four

Alan rode due south across the green plains. The wind was blowing over the grass making it look like waves on a malty colored ocean of green. He saw antelope a few buffalo and deer. He knew he was getting ready to enter indian country and he kept on the lookout for sign and movement. At around noon time Buddy murmured and pointed his ears forward. Alan pulled his Winchester 73 rifle across his lap at the ready. It turned out to be a couple of fur traders heading toward Wichita, Kansas, with four pack horses weighted down with bundles of furs of all kinds. They exchanged conversation for about ten minutes. They told Alan of seeing quite a few bands of indians but they didn't bother them and they just rode on their way with no confrontation taking place. Seemed like they all were heading north and set on going at a quick pace and didn't have time to mix things up. They told him they were mostly Shawnee and Comanche's. They also told him that were he was going he better be on the look out for Apaches and Cherokees. Alan thanked them for their information and the advice and bid them good day.

When he could, Alan tried to ride close to what available tree lines and gatherings of forest he could come in contact with. He wanted to get to Texas as soon as he could because he knew ranchers would be wanting to hire experienced cow hands and he didn't want to miss out. Besides the earlier he got there he could pick out the best paying ranches but he knew he had to be alert.

Alan rode on to near night fall and it would be getting dark quickly and he needed to find a good spot to camp and gather some good dry firewood. He saw a tree covered area with some large boulders and a stream running close by. Alan surveyed the area and picked a place to settle in. He took Buddy and the pinto mare to the stream to get a drink then tethered them to a couple of scrub oaks with plenty of grass for them to browse on. Alan gathered up some good dry hard wood and started to make a fire for coffee. He had some bacon and hardtack bread but wasn't to excited about the choice for his evening meal. He then noticed a hole under a boulder nearby. He thought that would be a good spot to research for some dinner fixin's. Maybe a rabbit or gopher turtle was in there, best to have a look. He poked a stick into the hole and heard a rattle. It was a western rattle snake. "Well dinner is taken care of." He thought to himself as he chuckled.

Alan cooked the snake on a forked stick and baked some arrow root he dug from the stream to back it up. A little salt sprinkled on both and he had a first class meal washed down with some hot coffee.

He checked out a good spot in the large rocks to make his bed for the night, carefully making sure there were no other snakes to be bothered with. Alan put down some pine boughs for bedding and placed his blanket on it. He then sat by the fire and rolled a smoke and sipped more coffee. "Can't get any better then this Buddy boy." He said. Buddy was probably thinking oats would be better. He sat and smoked his cigarette, finished his coffee grabbed his over coat for a night cover, smashed out his smoke and laid down for the night. He was about to doze off when he heard some splashing in the stream. He grabbed his Colt revolver and sat up at the ready. It turned out to be a couple of otters playing or chasing fish. "Maybe fish for breakfast." He considered. That would be tasty. Alan slept well only waking occasionally from an owl hoot or a coyote howling near by.

As day light came Alan found a long straight sapling and made a forked spear to catch a trout or two. After poking around here and there he had managed to get two nice trout about twelve inches long. He roasted them over the coals and had a good breakfast. Finishing his coffee he put out the fire and watered the horses and saddled up. He took a good look around to see if the coast was clear and headed south. He rode two days only stopping to water the horse when a stream was handy and grabbing some sleep. The second night he made camp after snagging a jack rabbit for diner. Eating dinner, drank coffee, rolled a smoke and hit the bedroll. He knew, or was pretty sure he was close to or was in Texas by now.

When he got up in the morning he would start looking for cattle or cowhands. Maybe he could hook up with a good paying ranch. He didn't get to far when he saw a light column of smoke coming from some trees a short distance away near a small steam. Not sure if it was an indian encampment he tethered the horses and decided to check it out. He crouched low and sneaked down for a closer look. There was a little clearing in the trees and he saw a small fire with a coffee pot sitting beside it and a tarp for a shelter. He studied the camp for a few minutes and thinking from the way it was set up it was not an indian camp but a camp made by a cowhand or two but he saw no one in the area. He thought about it for a minute and decided to walk into the camp to try and make contact but no one was in sight. As he stood there looking around he heard the click of a Henry or a Winchester rifle hammer being cocked behind him. The hair on the back of his neck bristled and he froze in place holding his hands out to be seen in a non threatening manner.

"Freeze an' don't turn around or I'll tag ya' fella." Someone ordered. It wasn't a hard manly voice but the softer voice of a woman. Possibly a young boy. Alan started to turn and the person behind him said, "Don't move unless I tell to move. Now lower those hands and unbuckle that gun belt an' let it drop."

Alan slowly reached down and unhooked his gun belt and let it drop to his feet. How did I get into this mess, he thought, how did I not see this ambush coming. After all these years being alert and on top of his game he was caught dead cold and where was this going?

"O K, now turn around slowly an' tell me who you are an' why your here."

Alan turned slowly and couldn't believe his eyes. In front of him was this young lady about five two, reddish blond hair, very shapely and oh my gosh good looking. She was beautiful!

She had a snug plaid shirt with buttons holding on for dear life and a pair of deer skin trousers that were earning every bit of their keep. She was holding a Henry lever action rifle with a silver plated barrel, pointed at him and the hole in

the barrel looked big enough to crawl into. What should he say?
"Cat got your tongue? I asked you a question."
"Ah, I'm sorry Miss, I mean ma'am, young lady, ah…. Well I didn't expect this. I mean out here in the middle of nowhere. I mean…"
"Stop your babbling an' get to the point. Ain't ya' never seen a woman before? Now start talking an' making some sense as I'm getting' mighty inpatient. Now who the hell are you an' why are you on my land?"
"Sorry ma'am I just didn't really expect to see such a lovely lady out here, I mean….."
"Shut up about the lady stuff cowboy, you men are all alike. I ain't falling for all that (bull manure). You telling me how sweet I look ain't gonna' work. I know I look decent so don't try to smooth me. Now step up here an' do some talking that makes sense or I'll just drill ya' an' get about my tasks, got a lot to do today."
Alan went to make a step forward and forgot about his gun belt around his feet and fell forward catching himself just as he came to the ground. The woman began to laugh. "First day with your new feet fella'?" She asked, and continued to laugh.
Alan felt like a fool. Never had he seen a woman this lovely in his life, but she was no fool either and she was in control of her surroundings and him also at the moment. This woman was really a special kind of woman, he thought!
"I'm sorry ma'am but…"

"OK let's cut the sorry line, you've said it way to many times. Now get to the point. Why are you on my land? Stealing more of my cows?"
"No ma'am, I didn't know I was on your land, in fact I don't know where I am, but I'm not out to steal any cows, I'm looking for work. I'm looking for a ranch that needs some help for the spring round up. I'm not a thief or a rustler; I'm a good and experienced cowhand."
"I could use some good help even you being a man an' all. But I don't know a thing about you."
"Ma'am I just finished a long hard cattle drive for a Mr. John Grisby Witt out of the Wyoming territory to Hayes City Kansas. I was the trail boss an' got those cattle there all safe an' sound. My name is Alan Holt."
"My name is Samara Halleck, so go get your horse an' let's sit an' talk over a cup of coffee and you can leave your gun belt right there."
Alan tipped his hat and went to get Buddy and the mare. When he returned Samara jumped up rifle in hand; "You no good low life lying thief." She shouted, "You're not a cattle rustler you're a horse thief. Oughta' shoot ya right now you lying skunk."
Alan looked at her in surprise and replied. "What do ya' mean?"
"That's my horse, disappeared two weeks ago. That means you've been here longer than you say. Knew I shouldn't have believed ya'. You're a man, Yall lie."
"Hold on lady let me explain. I didn't steal this mare, the indians that attacked me outside of Dodge had your horse when I killed them. One of the braves I killed was riding

your horse. Just let me explain and tell you about it. I have witnesses to back me up on what took place that night."

Samara shook her head. "OK sit down an' lie to me. But remember I got my rifle an' know very well how to use it, this better good."

"I don't lie ma'am. My Mom taught me that years ago as a youngin' with a razor strap."

Alan explained to Samara what happened the night he camped out side of Dodge City and how he caught the mare. She listened intently. "Glad I found her for you ma'am. I don't want her if she's yours and I'm happy to see you have her back."

Samara walked to the mare and snuggled her and patted her on the shoulder. "OK cowboy lets talk. Tell me about you an' what you can do."

Alan told her of his past, and about his cattle driving experiences as a drover and a trail boss. He told her of his background as a scout for the U. S. Cavalry for several years and he showed her his army papers, contacts, and army discharge. Samara was impressed, he seemed paper wise very qualified, but she didn't let him know that. He was a good looking man, strongly built and so funny bashful around women that made her chuckle inside. And then again he was a man, and they all lie, she thought, and couldn't be trusted. She based that on past experiences from dealing with men she encountered after her father was bushwhacked and killed a few years back. Samara had it rough now that her father was gone and every man she met after his passing has tried to take advantage of her. Samara listened to him as she drank her coffee. She had to think on this. Could a man be trusted? Could this one? He seemed honest enough, and maybe he would be a good man on the ranch. “Can you handle that gun you’re carrying?” She asked.

“Yes ma’am I can, and I’m handy with my rifle too!”

“Your gonna’ have be around here if you want to stay alive. There’s a lot going on in this neck of the woods for sure, and way to much lately.”

“All I’m asking of you ma’am is to give me a chance. I’ll prove my worth, and when I work I’m a one ranch man. I get the impression you don’t trust men but we are all not alike. The honest ones that is.”

Samara finished her coffee, set her cup down, and got up. She liked what she saw, but? She walked down to the creek. She had to think. He seemed honest enough but she trusted men before and it didn’t work out well. She needed competent help, that was certain, but she couldn’t afford another mistake. Samara stood there looking at the rippling stream, the sun light making the water sparkle like diamonds were on the surface. “Could this be the day that she finally met a man that could finally be trusted?” She thought to herself. Only heaven knew she needed such a man, but……?

Chapter Five

Alan stood and watched her wondering what she was thinking. “I might as well move on,” He thought to himself, “I have to find a job to earn enough money to add to what I have if I’m gonna’ buy my own ranch.”

He looked at her and she was standing now looking at him. “Ma’am,” Alan said, “I’m sorry I trespassed on your land. I am glad you got your horse back an’ if you’ll excuse me and let me pick up my gun belt I’ll be moving on. I’ll get off your property and continue to look for work elsewhere. Sorry to have inconvenienced you ma’am.” And he tipped his hat to her.

“No wait,” Samara answered, “Pick up your gun belt an’ let’s ride. You got a job, and I hope I’m right. I got some things I gotta’ check on, I’ll tell you what’s going on as we ride. Just don’t prove me a fool.”

Alan smiled. “Ma’am, I’ll give you my best and I’ll work as hard as if it was my ranch.”

Samara liked what she saw. “I’m putting you in charge. You’ll be the new ranch boss but you’re in for a surprise when you meet who you got working under you.”

Alan figured she had some not to experienced cowpokes and worthless drifters. But he’d deal with it.

They packed up her camp and mounted up.

“I’m losing cattle faster than I can round ‘em up.” She told him. “Don’t know exactly who’s doing it but I have an’ idea who’s behind it.”

“Have you reported it to the law?” Alan asked.

"No I haven't. Just can't prove anything yet, but I think I know who it is. There is a man named Mark Hayes, he has a ranch next to mine. Ever since my Dad was killed he has offered to buy me out several times, but I keep turning him down. I can't help but think he had something to do with Dad's death as he and my Dad had bad feelings against each other. One night after I told him to leave my ranch the barn was set a fire, burned most of our hay for the winter, an' the horses were scattered off."
"Sounds mighty suspicious." Alan said to her.
"Yea it does," Samara answered, "But like I told you there was no proof he did it. Then my drovers and ranch hands started disappearing, one here and there. A few of my help just got scared an' up and quit."
"How many do you have working for you now?"
"Only nine and that's not enough to help cover my herd."
"I'll see if I can recruit some men if you have a town near your ranch."
"The closest town is Hays Town, not much of a town, about tens miles away. But I don't know how many men you'll get as most are afraid of Mark Hayes. He pretty much runs the town and has the sheriff in his back pocket."
"One of those type of towns huh? After I get settled in an' meet who you have I'll give it a try. Might get lucky."
"I hope so. As I said I'm losing cattle every day."
"Well that's the first thing we gotta' stop ma'am."
"You better be very alert an' watchful Alan. It can't be indians, they only take one steer here an' there. I'd like to take a look around Mark's ranch; I'll bet I'd find some of my stock there."

“That’s one of the very next things I’m gonna’ do when I get some reliable help.”

“He’ll kill you Alan if he catches you on his land. You can bet on that.”

“He doesn’t know me ma’am or know I’m workin’ for you. I can go over there asking for work.”

“My Dad went to snoop around Mark Hayes ranch and was found dead not far from his property line. But again we couldn’t prove anything as Mark was in town playing cards. Said he didn’t know anything about it, you watch out for him.”

Samara didn’t know what made her take a chance on this man she never met, and just hired on, but she admired his background and his thinking. She needed a man that could handle himself and other men. “Can he handle Mark Hayes? Just hope I’m not wrong,” She thought.

“What are you out here looking for?” Alan asked.

“The other day some of my hands were rounding up strays on the west range and saw several men pushing cattle toward the Hayes ranch. My hands stayed out of sight as they were out numbered, but they said it looked like some of my cattle were in the herd they were pushing. So I’ve been out here for a couple of days to see what I could discover.”

“Were they Hayes ranch hands?” Alan asked.

“Not sure Alan. They could be, or they might have just been rustlers, trying to make a quick dollar. There are several bands of rustlers that have moved into the area lately. Some think Mark has brought a lot of them in.”

"From what you have been telling me, you shouldn't be out here alone."
"I can handle myself Mr. Holt, ain't my first trail ride."
Alan just shook his head in concern. Then asked; "Why does Mark want your ranch? Sounds like he has a big enough spread already?"
"Don't really know. He started pestering my Dad shortly after he took over the ranch from the Wyler's."
"Did the Wyler's sell out?"
"Mark said he did, showed a bill of sale supposedly signed by Tom Wyler after they found Tom dead."
"What did he die from?"
"Found him dead about a mile outside of Hays Town. Shot full of holes. The sheriff said it looked like a robbery as his money from the sale of the ranch was gone and anything else worth while was taken."
"Sounds mighty fishy, ma'am."
"Yes it does, but Mark Hayes was in town playing cards at the Black Steer Saloon bragging an' telling everybody about buying Tom Wyler out." Samara told Alan.
Alan was beginning to wonder what he had gotten himself into. A lot of questions to answer!
"Well Mr. Holt, lets ride back to the ranch an' I'll introduce you to the hands."

Chapter Six

Samara and Alan rode toward the ranch and as they went over a tall rise and the terrain changed from dry and arid buttes and mesa's to rolling hills and lush grassy plains with a couple of good sized streams running across . Cattle were everywhere; some had already dropping their calves.
"Are these all your cows' ma'am?"
"Most are, probably a few of some other ranches mixed in there."
"That's a big herd boss lady."
"Yes but I've lost about two hundred head in the last month. We gotta' stop it quickly. And the thing that bothers me is if we can't prove it's Hayes stealing 'em' the sheriff ain't gonna do a damn thing. I swear he's on Mark Hayes payroll."
"I'll do my best ma'am, I myself, can't stand a thief of any kind, and one with a badge…., that's as low as you can get."
"I agree Alan, and one more thing. You can stop with the ma'am stuff, bout had enough, call me Samara if ya will."
"How's about I just call ya Boss?"
"OK, I can handle that."
They rode on for a couple of miles and the ranch came into sight. "What a nice look-in' setup," Alan thought as he looked over how it was made up. Big ranch house, big bunk house and a newly built barn of considerable size. There were ranch hands sitting in front of the bunkhouse and several standing with a foot on the corral rails. The corral was large with some good looking horses in it.

"Here comes the boss lady an' a stranger." One of the help hollered and most of them, but a few, started to gather together to meet them.
"Boys, want ya ta' meet the new ranch boss, Alan Holt. He'll be run-in the show here under me from now on."
As they waved to greet him it struck him, "Boys, he thought to himself, almost all of them, but two, were women and quite a bunch of lookers to!" He turned and looked at Samara with surprise.
"Told ya you'd be surprised. After the mistrust in most men I started hiring these gal's. They can rope, drive, an' shoot if it has ta come to that. But most of all, I can trust 'em."
"Surprise doesn't quite say it boss." Alan answered. "Gonna' take some gettin' used too!" He turned back at the group and said, "Howdy men, nice to meet ya."
They all chuckled and snickered as they waved hello.
Get your horse settled en' meet me at the house." Samara told Alan. "I'm gonna' get washed up an' relax. You can wash up at the bunkhouse, I'm sure ya need it." She said laughingly and walked to the house. Alan stood there looking at her in those buckskin trousers, took a deep breath and walked Buddy to the corral. He pulled off Buddy's saddle and bridle, and then wiped Buddy down with a wet cloth before letting the big Grulla stallion in with the other horses. Buddy immediately went to work showing all who was boss in this circle and a couple of the mares started to check him over in approval. Buddy played hard to get, well for a minute or two that is.

Alan met the two men working there. One was the ranch carpenter, Phil Burd, and the other was an aging cowpuncher named Windy Lee. Alan asked how they could work with all these women and they told him they were just a bunch of tomboys and he'd get used to it. Alan asked where they washed up and Windy pointed at the bunkhouse and told Alan there were tubs in there. Alan went to the bunkhouse and went about looking for how to get some hot water made up to bathe in. As he was preparing his fixins' a tall nice looking gal walked in. She was about five foot eight, and everything about her body was in just the right place. She was lovely. Alan stopped what he was doing and took a good hard look. "This jobs gonna' be a tough one." He thought.

"Howdy Boss, need any help?" She asked.

"Well I could use some buckets of hot water and a tub, young lady."

"We got some water heating up in that big tank just out side as we gal's all get washed up before dinner. My names Haley Hurst, I'll be happy to pitch in. Let me show you how we do it." She went to a side door and pushed it open. There were five tubs with a pipe running across the back of them with a faucet at each tub.

"Just turn that knob at the tub an' fill ere' up." Haley told him.

"Thank you young lady," Alan answered, "If you'll excuse me I'll get started."

"Need any help?" Haley asked Alan with a smile on her face.

"I think I can handle it from here," Alan replied, "Thanks though."
"Tis' a shame." Haley said walking out closing the door behind her. Alan shook his head and started making his hot bath. The hot water and soap felt good. He lathered up and shaved and washed his hair, it was so nice to relax. He laid there with his head back and closed his eyes.
Suddenly the door opened and a short perky black-haired gal walked in, towel and clothes over her arm.
"Scuse' me Boss, gotta get washed up before the rush. Names Hannah, Hannah Noel, nice ta' meet ya." She said. "Yall just look the other direction en' I'll take that tub at the far side."
Alan thought, "This is really going to take some doing to get used to this. And just how do I get out of the tub?"
Hanna filled her tub and got in singing as she washed not looking his way. Alan finished washing and grabbed for his towel to get out. Just as he got out of the tub the door flew open and two more gal's walked in. They stood there looking at Alan, both just wearing a smile and a towel over their arm. Alan quickly wrapped his towel around him, trying not to stare. He hurriedly went for the sleeping area where his clothes were laid out. Alan could hear them giggling in the tub area. He took a deep breath and quickly got dressed. "How am I gonna' sleep here?" He wondered.

Chapter Seven

Alan got dressed combed his hair, wiped his boots and went to the main house. It was a nice home with a nice front porch equipped with rocking chairs. A big brindle dog was lying by the front door. Alan walked to the door to knock and the big dog growled at him, Alan stopped.
"Shut up Buster!" Samara hollered, "Don't mind him Alan, his bark is more dangerous than his bite. Unless you fool with his food, that is. Come on in."
Alan carefully walked by Buster, and Buster sniffed at his feet, snorted and walked off the porch.
"You clean up pretty good fella,' you meet some of the help?"
"Yes I did, gonna' take a while to get used to working with them."
"They're tough, just treat 'em as the boys, they'll work for you OK. How about a drink? "
"Don't mind if I do ma'am, I mean Boss."
Samara smiled and poured Alan a drink of bourbon and one for herself.
"Dinner will be around six. Sit and relax, take your boots off if you like, I ain't wearing mine." She said to him and wiggled her bare feet.
"I'll keep my boot's on Boss, after all these years kinda' used to wearing them all the time."
"Suit yourself; I can't wait to get out of mine. Have a seat an' let's talk business while we're waiting for Molly to finish dinner. You are going to eat aren't ya?" She asked him and pointed to a chair.

"Yes boss if you don't mind. Ain't had a home cooked meal in a while."

Alan was impressed with the house and furnishings. Big dinning table, leather stuffed couch and matching chairs in the living area. Several stuffed animal heads on the wall, deer, elk, bison, antelope and an enormous bear with it's mouth open showing big teeth. There were several rifles on the wall, including a finely made Pennsylvania flint lock long rifle.

They sat and Samara told Alan as they sipped on their drinks, what was going on and her trouble with Mark Hayes and the loss of cattle. She told him they had spotted several strangers riding on her property as of late. Samara also again told Alan again that she thought that Mark had a lot to do with what was going on. The barn burning, her father's death, cattle losses and the men leaving her ranch. She told Alan that she started hiring the women because of her mistrust of men and the way men tried to maneuver her.

Alan told her that as soon as he could get settled in and become familiar with the ranch he would start trying to come to a solution. He also told her that he was going to try hire some men he could trust if there was any.

Samara told him, "That's most likely gonna' be tough, as Mark pretty much controls what happens in this part of the country, even the law, meaning the sheriff. And don't you worry about the gals here, Alan, they can shoot well and handle themselves."

"But they are women boss. Are they tough enough to fight? I mean hardened?"

"Alan they came to me because they were at the end of their rope and needed work to survive. A couple of those gals in a fight I wouldn't guarantee you'd win that contest. Some of them can fight hard as a man."

"That's good to know Boss."

"Dinners ready Miss Halleck," Molly called out, "Whenever you're ready."

Samara and Alan walked to the table and sat down. Samara said grace before the meal. It was roast duck, sweet potatoes and peas. "All this came from our ranch." Samara told Alan. "Phil does all the planting and everyone helps care for the vegetables. Some of the gals are good at canning so we have plenty for the winter months."

Alan enjoyed his meal, and Molly brought out a pie made from cactus fruit, it was very tasty. When they finished they went out on the porch to sit in the rockers and Alan rolled a smoke. He told Samara he was going to ride to the Hayes ranch and have a look around in the morning.

"I wouldn't do that Alan," she told him, "He's likely to kill you."

"No ma'am, as I told you, I'm going to see him about a job an' how much he pays. My thought is, one, I can have a look at some of the cattle when I ride in, and two, it will give me an' idea how much to offer the men in town, if it's OK with you?"

"Just be very careful Alan," Samara said, "Don't want to lose ya on your first day."

"Well boss, he doesn't know me from Adam. So I can ride in there ask about work and tell him I'll let him know. It'll give me time to look around and Mark not knowing I work for you, he won't be suspicious. I think it'll work fine."

"Just watch out Alan, he's no dummy. Tomorrow morning before you go I'll introduce you to all the crew. Why don't you go get your gear and put 'em in the back bedroom here, don't want ya' to be attacked by the gals in your sleep tonight." She said with a smile. "You'll have everything you'll need in there. It used to be my Dad's room. Oh, and don't worry, I'll lock my door." She said laughingly.

Alan was surprised, he didn't expect that offer. He went to the bunkhouse and gathered his gear to take back to the main house.

"Where ya' going boss?" One of the girls asked. "We was looking ta havin' ya' spend the night here!" All the gals laughed at that remark and as much as he was surprised by Samara's offer to stay at the main house, he was relieved to get out of there. Too tempting, he thought. He went to the back bedroom and took off his shirt and boots to get ready to hit the bed. Samara locked the front door and passed by the room, the door was slightly ajar. She saw him standing there with his shirt off and it showed his muscular build. He was not a big man, just short of six feet, but he had a good strong, and firm build. "He's a good looking man." She thought. Samara took a deep breath and went to her room. She laid in bed and couldn't get the vision of him out of her mind. "Stop," Samara thought to herself, "I'm not looking for a man. I'm looking for a foreman." She rolled over but it was hard to get the sight of him from her mind.

Chapter Eight

Alan awoke at daybreak, and got dressed. He stepped into the main room and saw Molly in the kitchen, she waved at him. Samara's door was still closed. Alan went out on the porch and rolled a smoke, then walked over to the corral to check on Buddy. Buddy seemed to have a grin on his face and was surrounded by mares. Alan called to him and Buddy gave Alan a look like, "I'm a little busy right now," And just stood there. Alan called him again and Buddy walked to him seemingly reluctant. Alan rubbed Buddy's nose and neck. "You happy big boy?" Alan asked Buddy. "Better go say your excuse me's as we got some work to do today." Alan rubbed Buddy's chest and looked over toward the bunk house and saw the help was making coffee and something to eat.

"Breakfast is ready Mr. Holt, the boss lady is waiting." Molly called out to him.

"Better not keep ere' waitin'." One of the gals said loudly and other all chuckled. Old man Windy pointed to the house, a grin on his face.

Alan went to the house and stepped in.

"Come sit an' eat," Samara said, "Hope you like pancakes an' bacon."

"Sure do boss." Alan replied, pulled out a chair across from Samara.

"Alan, I want you to be very careful today going to the Hayes ranch. He is not stupid and he's fast to use his guns."

“I’ll be OK boss, he won’t have any idea that I didn’t just ride in today and I’ll get to see some of the herd an’ check brands.”

“I’m sure you’ll find some of my cattle there,” Samara said, “But I don’t know what we’re gonna’ be able to do about it. He’s got a lot of men and not all of them are drovers.”

“You said we can’t trust the sheriff, but maybe we can get a U.S. Marshal out here.”

“You’ll have to go clear to the town of Canadian to send a telegram, can’t send it from Hays Town. And if Mark gets wind of it, it’ll start a war between our two ranches. I just hope you got a good plan as we don’t need a war with him.”

“Boss lady, he’s been pushing you around long enough an’ I aim to put a end to it so you can start back to making money on this ranch.” Alan told her.

They finished their breakfast and Samara took Alan outside to officially meet the ranch hands.

“OK everyone gather up.” Samara hollered.

The gals, Windy and Phil all got together.

“I want ya’ll to meet the new boss, Alan Holt, an’ I want ya to come up an’ shake his hand when I call your name.”

“If you put up your hand, I’ll come to you.” Alan said to them.

“OK then,” Samara said, “Alan meet Haley Hurst.” Haley smiled and said, “We’ve met yesterday,” and reached out her hand.

Then Samara said, "This is Kaycee Britt, Macy Allen, Hannah Noel, Sabrina Zeager, Lisa Moody, Nicole Martin, Phil Burd, Brooke Allen, Shelby Dykes and Windy Lee."
Alan walked down the line and shook each of their hands. Then he stepped back and said. "Nice to meet you all. I want you all to go about your daily choirs for a couple of days while I have a look around. After I get a sight on things we will start working together. Thank you!"
"OK folks," Samara said, "Lets get ta' work."
"OK boss'" Alan said, "I'm gonna' get saddled up and ride to the Hayes ranch then go on to Hays Town an' see if I can get a couple of hands. Might just spend the night an' be back tomorrow, with some help I hope."
"You be careful Alan, very careful." Samara said and patted him on the back.
Alan got his gear, saddled up Buddy and asked Phil how to reach the Hayes ranch. Phil told Alan to head southwest about twelve miles and start looking for the ranch house. Alan thanked Phil and Phil said "Be on yer' toes my boy, an' good luck."

Chapter Nine

Alan rode across some very lush grassland with cattle spread out everywhere. Some of the cattle had Samara's H Bar brand and some had circle H brands. Also there was a mixture of other brands. Alan thought with the ranches next to each other the two brands would be mixed here. When he got to the ranch the true story would be told. .It was some beautiful country and the sun shining on the mountains on the horizon were showing beautiful colors of all shades. There was a refreshing breeze and the air was fresh and clear. After traveling to about noon Buddy murmured and perked his ears forward. Alan pulled Buddy up as he knew Buddy had sensed something. Indians, Mountain lion? It didn't take but a few minutes before Alan saw four riders coming his way. At this point he didn't know whose ranch he was on. He released the thong over his pistol hammer for a quick draw if needed.

The riders rode to Alan and pulled up their horses. They were a hard looking group.

"What ya' doing fella?" One of them, a tough looking cold eyed man asked.

"Met a prospector back a piece an' he said the Hayes ranch might be hiring. Do you know how to find that ranch, I'm lookin' for work."

"Got any cow experience? Can ya' handle a gun?"

"Ya, I can do both, if the wage is good enough." Alan replied.

"Follow us, we was headin' to the ranch house when we saw ya' a ridin' here." The man told Alan.

They rode several miles at a good gate and then Alan saw a big ranch house and a large barn not far off. They rode up to the house and a man was sitting on the porch.
Tell the boss a man wants ta' see 'em." The tough guy told the man on the porch, and the man went inside.
Only a few seconds went by and this huge, tall, hawked faced man stepped out on to the porch. He had long white blond hair, six foot five and weighed at least two hundred and fifty pounds. He was a big tough looking man that could surely handle himself. Alan tried not to look surprised. He had gunfighter's eyes, just slits glaring at Alan. He wore two colts with ivory handle grips, worn low, tied down and he obviously knew how to handle them.
"Where ya' from?" He asked Alan.
"From up Kansas way." Alan replied. "Some say you might be hiring good experienced hands."
"Might be," The big man said, "If you're any good that is."
"I can hold my own sir, how much ya' payin'?"
"Forty dollars a month, plus eats an' a bunk. That's more than you'll get anywhere else around here. And stay clear of the Halleck ranch, that woman can't pay herself! Besides, won't be long a fore I own that ranch too."
"That sounds like a fair wage an' some good advice" Alan said, "Let me ride into town an' ponder it over a drink. I'm a little dry an' tired, been a long ride."
"Let me know soon, just about got all the hands I need," The big man said, "Names Mark, Mark Hayes, don't dally around if you want work for a good wage." He turned and went back into the house.

“Thanks for your help fella’s. Which way is town, not very familiar with this part of the country.”
One of the men pointed in the westerly direction, Alan tipped his hat at him and started riding to Hays Town. As he rode on he saw several cows with the H Bar brand. He also saw cattle that the H Bar brand had been changed to Circle H brand. That’s what he was looking for.
Alan rode into Hays Town. It wasn’t much of a town, a saloon, a small sheriff’s office, a store, a blacksmith shop and a few houses.

Historical note; The settlement of Hays Town, Texas, was started by E.C. Hays after he built a store there at the crossing of two roads. Hays Town changed its name to Spearman after a Santa Fe Railroad owner in 1917.

Alan rode up to the hitching rail at the Black Steer Saloon and tied Buddy off and entered through the swinging doors. There were a few cowhands at the bar and a few sitting at tables, some playing cards, and others just talking. The saloon was owned by Don Volsch and his wife, Terri. It was clean and tidy and had the head of a big black longhorn steer on the back wall behind the bar. Don was tending bar and walked over to Alan.
“How ya’ doing friend?” Don asked.
“Doing OK, I’ll take a shot of rye.”
“We got some real good aged corn an’ cactus whisky if you’d like to try it.” Don told Alan. “Aged a year in oak kegs.”
“OK, let my give it a try, make it yourself?”

"No we get it from a man that lives a couple of miles from here. Think you'll like it. It's been a good seller here. The boys really like it." Don answered and poured Alan a glass. "Just ridin' through?"
"No I got me a job running a ranch near here and looking for some good cowhands. What's my chances?"
"You ain't working for Hayes are ya'?" Don asked. "Thought he had a good man running his place, not saying you're not good though."
"No I'm working for the Halleck ranch," Alan replied, "I'm needin' a couple of experienced men if any is available."
"You got to be kidding fella' ain't nobody around here gonna' go to work there. And if you got any sense you'll move on while you still can." Don said to Alan.
"Why do you say that?"
"For a bunch of reasons my friend." Don replied. "First, she's a Spitfire Mustang, killed her husband and a gal that worked here dead as a door nail right there on those stairs a couple of years ago." Don said pointing at the stairway that went to the second floor. "And not to long ago she killed her fiancé and another gal an' got away with both killings' free an' clear."
"I didn't know about that." Alan said.
"And reason number two, my friend," Don said, "That Halleck woman an' Mark Hayes been a feuding ever since her Dad's death. Get in his way son an' he'll kill ya."
"Who killed her Dad?" Alan asked.
Don leaned over the bar to Alan and whispered, "Don't go asking questions if you enjoy breathing."

Chapter Ten

At this point the saloon was silent; you could hear a pin drop and all eyes were on Alan.

A man at the bar walked over to Alan and said lightly, "Boy you just might have bit off more than you can chew. Take his advice," nodding at Don, "An, light out of here while you still can." He patted Alan on the shoulder and turned back to his friends.

"Terri," Don said, "Watch the bar for me," Then said pointing to a table, "Lets sit down my man and let me fill you in."

Don told Alan that Samara was getting suspicious of her husband cheating on her, after a couple of months marriage. His coming to town often got her ere, so she decided to check up on him. Samara caught him and a woman who worked for our saloon coming down the stairway arm an arm and Samara confronted him. The woman pulled out a derringer, pointed at Samara, and Samara pulled her pistol and shot them both in the chest. Samara was taken to trial on two counts of murder but the judge ruled it was a crime of passion and heart break, self defense, and he acquitted her on both charges.

Her fiancé and a gal from town was found dead in a meadow outside of town. Her fiancé was lying on top of the gal and they both were killed by the same bullet fired from a hillside above them. Everyone figured Samara did it but there was not, according to the sheriff, any evidence to prove it and all at the ranch said Samara was there all day.

Alan's head was spinning but as he thought about it he didn't blame Samara for doing it, after all she was being cheated on! Alan asked Don again who he thought killed Samara's dad.

"I got a good idea," Don said, "But I'm keeping my mouth shut and if I were you I wouldn't go nosing around and asking about it. Not in this town pal."

Alan glanced around and it seemed all in the saloon were talking in a whisper. He asked Don, "Do you think I will be able to get a couple of men? I'm offering a good wage."

"Doubt it my man," Don answered, "Most around here work for Mark and not all of them are cowpunchers, if you get my meaning, an' those that don't work for him, a lot of them worked for that gal but quit out of fear of Mark."

"Can I get a room for the night here?" Alan asked.

"Ya' but after what all have heard here today lock your door an' sleep with your pistol in your grip." Don answered.

Alan thanked Don for the information, shook his and told him he would be back for a meal and a room at evening time. He walked outside and walked Buddy to the blacksmith shop and asked the man there if could put Buddy up for the night. The man told Alan to put Buddy in the corral and he would feed him a bait of grain and hay before he closed.

As Alan walked around the small town any man that he walked toward or near turned from him as not to have noticed him. Alan walked to the store to have a look around inside and when he entered the man behind the counter

greeted him. "Howdy fella heard you're walkin' round in a pit of rattlesnakes." He said.
"News travels fast." Alan answered.
"Don't take long in a town this small ole' buddy. Seems like I heard you been looking for help. You ain't most likely gonna' find none around here though."
"Seems that way," Alan replied, "But I'm going to at least ask around."
"Ask all ya' want my friend but I doubt you'll have any luck. This thing with Hayes an' the Halleck girl gonna' end up with some killin' I'm afraid."
"Is that why the towns named after him, he runs it?"
"The town is named after me, E.C. Hays, we ain't no relation an' his name is spelled with a E in it. But you're about right, he runs this town alright, an' Sheriff Tom Crone does what ever Mark tells him. Used to be a nice quiet little town till Mark showed up an' bought Wyler out."
"I've heard there might be more to that story if the truth was known." Alan said.
"Better not go poking your face in that hole my friend. I'd stay way clear of asking around about that. Might get bit, real dead like. Mark Hayes has a bill of sale signed by Wyler but the money, if there was any, disappeared in a robbery."
"Sounds mighty fishy to me Mr. Hays."
"You can smell the fish all ya' want, my man, but don't go trying to find out where the odor is coming from."

“Thanks for the information, Mr. Hays, If you have anyone coming in looking for a good paying job, tell them to look me up at the Black Steer.”
“I’ll do that fella, and watch your back.”
Alan walked over to the blacksmiths shop and watched him make a couple of horse shoes, walked over and patted Buddy and went back to the Black Steer Saloon. Terri, Don’s wife was tending bar. She was a very attractive lady with eyes that sparkled and a nice smile.
“Let me have a shot of you house whisky,” Alan asked, “It has a good flavor to it.”
“It’s a good seller,” Terri replied as she poured a heavy shot, “The men really like it, it’s a little to strong for me though. Don said you wanted a room tonight, so I got room two ready for you, here’s the key.”
“Thanks ma’am.”
The saloon was doing a good business, cowmen, miners, and freight men, coming and going, getting drinks and some playing cards or having a meal at the tables. Alan figure all must have blown over as they weren’t looking at him as they were earlier. Terri told Alan the house special was pork and black beans with hot rolls and to just let her know when he was ready to eat. Alan asked Terri if any strangers came if she could ask them if they were looking for work, and if they did, come to see him in the morning. She told Alan, “We get a few driftin’ through at night stopping for a drink. If they look honest enough, I’ll ask ‘em.”

With that Alan told Terri he was ready to eat his meal and go to bed. Terri smiled and told him to pick a table and she would have his meal in a couple of minutes.

The meal was very good, the pork was seasoned just right and the hot rolls with butter set the meal off. After eating Alan finished his coffee and was ready to go to get some rest. He thanked Terri, left a tip on the table and climbed the stairs to his room. He took off his boots, then sat on the bed and rolled a smoke. He was wondering what he had got himself into but the more he thought about how much help Samara needed the more he felt right. After enjoying his smoke he opened the window some to let fresh air in the room. He turned, dropped his trousers, pulled off his shirt and climbed into bed. As he laid there he thought of Samara, "She's a lovely woman," He said to himself, "But I don't see her getting hopped up over any man soon, but she is such a woman."

Alan didn't go off to sleep right away. He thought about his chanced of finding a couple of good men and of how he was going to confront Mark Hayes. Some how he's got to get a lawman to look this over. A U. S. Marshal would be such a man if he can find one. But in the meantime he did need some dependable help. He pulled up his sheet and as closed his eyes all he could see was Samara.

Chapter Eleven

Alan got up washed his face and hands, went down stairs to have breakfast. Terri came over and poured Alan a cup of coffee.

"Some strangers came in last night and this morning, Mr. Holt, but they were not looking for work, just moving through."

"Thank you ma'am," Alan said, "I guess I'm not gonna' get any help from these parts. Might have to go all the way to Canadian, Texas to find some men."

"That's a long ride," Terri said, "Over fifty miles, do you want some breakfast?"

"I'll have some pancakes and a slice of smoked ham if you have any."

"Yes we do, it'll be out in a minute."

As Alan sipped on his coffee, three men came in and walked up to the bar. Don asked if he could help them.

"They say there's a guy here lookin' for some help," One of them said, "He around?"

That caught Alan's attention and he glanced over to the bar and didn't believe his eyes. It was an old friend he met when serving for the Calvary and they worked a few drives together, it was Sam Griffin. He was a good looking well built man, nearly six foot tall and short brown hair. Sam was a good shot and could handle himself in a fight also. He had two strong looking, well built young men with him.

"Sam, Sam Griffin," Alan called out, "How the hell are you friend?"

Sam turned and recognized Alan immediately.

"Alan, ole buddy," Sam said, "Good to see ya' pal, you the man hiring?"
""That's me Sam, have a seat an' some coffee."
Sam walked over to Alan's table and introduced his two companions.
"This here is Ronnie Hall and Greg Bledsoe, a couple of friends of mine, we've been working together for a couple of years up in Kansas, an' thought we'd try Texas for a change of scenery. Just can't imagining running into you down here."
The three of them sat down at Alan's table, ordered coffee and meals. Alan told Sam of his last job driving a herd to Hays City, Kansas with the Witt's ranch from the Wyoming Territory. Alan and Sam talked about their times together for a while, then he told them about the Halleck ranch and what was going on there and the trouble with Mark Hayes. Alan told them there would be trouble and most likely some gun play involved before it's over because some of the men at the Hayes ranch were not hired on to punch cows.
"We ain't afraid of gun play." Ronnie replied.
"Not a bit." Greg added.
"I want to tell you men," Alan said, "I need good experienced help, and I could use you, but there's a big chance your gonna' get shot up or even killed. And with you being a good friend Sam, I just can't be comfortable putting you or your buddy's lives in danger."
"Are you saying if we were strangers that would be OK then Alan?" Sam asked. "It's OK to kill strangers?"

"No I don't mean it like that," Alan replied, "I don't want to see anyone get hurt. I need help, I'm trying to help Samara protect and save her ranch, but you bring up a good point. At what price? I'm willing to fight to help her, but to risk any life……? Well I guess that's what's wrong. He's got hired gunman working there."
"Sounds like your life is already in jeopardy and a good friend can't allow his buddy to go it alone. I think I can speak for Ronnie an' Greg, you can count us in."
"You bet!" Ronnie and Greg said in unison. "Count us in."
B sides ain't had no gun play for weeks." Ronnie said.
"Not since them Apaches tried to bush us a couple days ago."
"Don't forget them two in Dodge City." Greg replied. "We handled them OK."
Alan thanked them for their support and shook each mans hand.
Then Sam said to Alan. "You'd do the same for me fella', Besides we can't wait to meet the help, we can help ya' take care of them too."
"Oh I can see we ain't gonna get anything done now," Alan said laughingly, "Yall' be chasing women, not cows or rustlers."
"Not during daylight." Greg answered and they all laughed.
As they were finishing breakfast a tall young man walked into the saloon, went to the bar and ordered a shot of whiskey. He drank it down in a gulp and ordered another. As the bartender was pouring he saw Alan at the table.

“Ain’t you the guy at the ranch yesterday lookin’ for work?” He said looking at Alan.
“You’re right fella’, that was me.”
“Better not wait to long as the boss has just about enough men to do what he needs to do.”
“Well thanks,” Alan answered, “I got a couple of friends joining me and we’ll meet real soon, that’s for sure.”
“Boss might not need your friends.”
“These are special men, he’ll meet them alright.” Alan told him.
“Better be good gunmen, got enough cow men.” He downed his drink and walked out. Don at the bar told Alan. “That was Hunter Hurst, working for Mark Hayes, and his sister is Haley Hurst, she’s working for you at the Halleck ranch. Tis’ a strange situation for sure.”
Alan thanked Don, then told Sam what he had rode over to check out Marks ranch and to see how many of the Halleck cattle were there. Then he asked Sam, “With the size of the ranch that Mark had gotten from Tom Wyler why did he want Samara’s ranch so badly. He has plenty of range, cattle, water and forest. How much more did he need and why?”
“Greed, or maybe he just wants to be the controlling cattleman in this part of Texas,” Sam replied, “If a rail head comes this way the big guys are going to control it all.”
“You might be right Sam, I also thought of that. But it could be something you and I don’t know about yet, something on the Halleck land he wants.” Alan told Sam.
“Could be Alan, we’ll have to look around. Maybe there’s a gold mine there.” Sam said then laughed.

"Let me pay my bill an I'll meet ya' out front an' take ya' to the ranch."

Alan paid Don and thanked him for his information.

Alan met Sam, Greg and Ronnie out front of the Black Steer and they walked over to the livery to get Buddy. Alan paid the man and saddled up. They rode off heading for the Halleck ranch. The problem was there were no open roads to the Halleck Ranch from Hays Town, and they had to cross the Hayes Ranch property to get there. This made Alan a little tense. He told the men riding with him to be on look out for Hayes riders but he knew full well they were already thinking about that.

It was going to be nearly a half day ride before they got there and it was hot and dusty as it hadn't rained for days. About a hour out they saw a cloud of dust but were not sure if it were people or cattle. They all pulled up and Alan got out his binoculars from his saddle bag to see if he could make out the cause of the dust. After a minute he saw it was five men riding west. As they got closer they spotted Alan's group and headed in their direction.

"Most likely Hayes men," Alan said, "Best be ready for trouble." And with that they all released the thong that tethered their pistols in their holsters. Sam pulled his rifle and sat it across his lap.

The men rode up to them and spread out a little.

"What ya' doin'," A big man on a pinto asked.

"Just passin' through." Alan answered, "Hope to get to Wolf Creek by noon. then follow it to Indian Territory."

(Oklahoma was known than by that name.)

“Well ya better head more north. Way yer’ goin’, yer’ gonna’ miss Wolf Creek all ta’ gether.”
“Oh, OK, thanks, new to this country. Didn’t realize we were headin’ the wrong way.” Alan answered. “Thanks for the help.”
“Ain’t I seen you afore’ pardner’?” One of the Hayes men asked, a young man with a squinted left eye
“Was at the Black Steer for a drink an’ a meal yesterday, then moved on.”
“Ain’t you the one that was lookin’ for help?”
“Nope, not me. Me an’ my friends here headin to do some prospecting.”
“That’s Injun territory my friend,” The man on the pinto said, “Yall might loose some yer’ hair.”
“We can handle Indians,” Sam replied.
“I tell ya Mark, they ain’t no prospectors, their russlers’. He was trying to get some cowmen back in Hays.” The man with the squint said.
“You wouldn’t know a prospector from preacher.” The man on the pinto said. He turned to Alan and told him to head north to find Wolf Creek, turned his horse and told his men to ride.
“Well that turned out better than I had hoped.” Sam said.
“Ya it did, Sam, lets get movin’.” Alan answered, and they continued on. Just past noon they rode into the Halleck Ranch yard. Phil and Windy were working on the corral. Samarra heard them ride in and she came out to meet them. She looked very lovely. Alan introduced Sam, Ronnie, and Greg and she nodded at them.
“Looks like you found some help.” She said.

“Ya’ boss, an old friend of mine, and his buddies” Alan replied, “Got a lot to tell ya’.”
“Get the men settled in, freshen up an’ meet me at the house Alan.” She waved at them and went back to the house.
“Wow, Mr. Alan,” Greg said, “Is that the boss?”
“Yep it is but don’t get any plans about that woman,” Alan said, “She’ll kill ya’ or maybe I will.” Alan chuckled.
Sam, Ronnie and Greg looked at Alan with a grin and shook their heads. Alan showed them around, introduced them to the help that was around the yard and then got cleaned up and walked to the house.
“Make sure you got work on your mind.” Sam said and the others laughed.

Chapter Twelve

Alan went into the house and Samara greeted him with a drink in her hand and gave it to him.
"How'd it go Alan?"
"I went to the Hayes Ranch boss and saw a lot of our cattle there. Some with the brands changed. Gotta' get a Marshal out here and have him take a look around. Ain't no doubt where those cattle came from. When the Marshal looks around there he'll have enough to hang Mark."
"If Mark don't kill him first Alan. By the way, I'm glad you're back safe an' sound."
"You were worried about me Boss?"
"Nonsense, just worried about you safety and concerned for the ranch's success. Sure glad you ran into your friend and his pals, we need 'em."
Alan thought about that for a minute, 'maybe she was worried about him'.
"They are going to work out well Boss and they are eager to get started."
"What do you have in plan Alan?"
"Gonna get all the hands out after breakfast and have them push all the cattle close to the Hayes Ranch line back deeper into our pastures. Gonna' have them split up into three groups. One group north, one group south and the other group to the west. That will make it harder for Marks men to gather up anymore of our stock."
"That sounds like a good plan, Alan, that will cut down on the losses. I tried that several times but the gals were run off."

“I don’t think there going to run us anymore Samara, those boys an’ me will be there to handle the Hayes men this time.”

“Great, Alan, sounds like we can finally get a break.”

“Sam and his friends won’t be pushed around. I know Sam is good with a gun and Ronnie an’ Greg appear to be a pair to be reckoned with.”

“I hope no one gets hurt Alan, I worry about that and how are you going to get the U.S. Marshal out here? You can’t send a telly from Hays Town.”

“Can old man Windy still ride well?’

“He’s a good hand Alan, not as fast as he once was, but yes he can ride well and he knows the territory very well. Why do you ask?”

“I’m going have him ride to Canadian tomorrow. He can send it from there. If he leaves in the morning he can be there by noon. I’ll talk to him tonight.”

“I just hope we can get a Marshal here quickly Alan.”

Alan asked how long it would be until dinner, and Samara said it would be ready in about an hour, so he excused himself to go talk to the help of his plans for tomorrow.

Most all the ranch hands were in the yard talking in small groups. Alan walked up to Haley Hurst and asked her to get all the gals over by the fire near the corral. Sam, Ronnie, Windy, Greg and Phil were sitting around that small fire cooking coffee and talking. Haley brought the gals to the fire. “Gottem’ all but two Boss,” Haley said, “Lisa an’ Nicole should be ridding in any moment.”

“Thanks Haley. OK men, pardon me ladies, here’s what we gotta’ do tomorrow!”

Alan laid out his plan of gathering the herd into a tighter group closer to the ranch so they could keep a closer eye on them and stop the rustling of cattle in the far out pastures and near the Hayes ranch border.
"That's over eight hundred head of cattle!" Phil commented.
"If we have to we will go out again the next day and the next after that." Alan answered. "We gotta get those cattle to where we can watch them until we get the legal help I'm sending for. And if we have to, and I think we will, we'll go on Hayes land if we see cattle with our brand on them. They can't say a thing about that"
Alan also warned them that there was a chance there would be trouble and to make sure they had there pistols and rifles loaded and ready. He told the women to use which gun they handled best and to let the man in charge of each group make the decisions and do the talking.
"Remember lady's," Alan said, "It's not how fast you are its how straight you shoot."
"They all can shoot straight." Alan turned and saw Samara had walked up behind him to where they all were standing.
"We have practiced shooting a lot Alan, an' these gals can handle themselves."
"That's good Boss, lets just hope it doesn't come to that. Sam, you take the west side. Ronnie you take the north range, an' Greg, you ride with me to the south side."
"I'll ride with you Alan," Samara told him, "Greg, you can go with one of the others."
"I don't want you out there Boss lady. You'll be safe to sit here."

“Not a chance Alan, I fight for my ranch right next to my help. We are all in this together and I’m not gonna’ sit idly by. If there’s trouble I can’t expect them to face all the danger for me. I’m gonna’ be right next to them and that’s it, discussion closed.” The whole gathering cheered Samara. Alan shook his head, he didn’t want her endangered, but he knew he was not going to talk her out of it. He then turned to Windy.

“Windy I want you to move out at daybreak an’ ride to Canadian to send a telegram for me. I’ll write it out so all you have to do is deliver it.”

“Boss man, I’ll do better then that,” Windy answered, “I’ll be a pullin’ out at four in the morn. That a’ way I’ll be a givin’ it to ‘em as soon as that there office opens.”

“Great Windy, that will be just great. And Windy, I want you to wait for the reply so we know what we got.”

“Will do Boss, will do fer’ sure.” And he shook Alan’s hand.

Alan went over the plan again with all and asked them to be ready to ride at daybreak. They all agreed and went to wash and have dinner.

“Come on to the house, dinner will be ready soon, so let’s have drink before dinner.” Samara said to Alan, and they walked to the house. As they sat having their drink Alan told Samara he really wanted her to stay at the ranch out of danger, but he could see that wasn’t going anywhere, she flatly refused. Alan and Samara had a very nice dinner of fried chicken prepared by Molly the cook. Molly was a round black lady of considerable size, and always smiling

and cheerful. If there was something Molly was sure of, she could cook.
Alan and Samara sat on the porch after dinner, with buster laying next to them, and talked for about an hour. Then Alan excused himself and went to see Buddy and give him some bread. Alan was thinking of how lovely Samara was. She was truly beautiful. The thoughts of her getting injured really bothered him. He then went and talked a while with Sam, making sure all was in place for tomorrow, and went back to the house to turn in for the night. Alan bid Samara good night.
"See you in the morning ma'am." He said and tipped his hand at her.
"I'll have Molly get breakfast ready early Alan. See ya' in the morning. Good night an' sleep well."
"Will do Boss, will do."
Alan went to his room leaving his door ajar so he could hear if any movement took place in the house while he was sleeping. It was something he had done for years, always being alert for danger. Alan kicked his boots off, removed his shirt and went to the wash basin to rinse his hands and face. As he was drying his face he looked in the mirror and noticed Samara was standing outside his room looking at him through the partially opened door and he went to turn. Samara saw that he noticed her and she was suddenly embarrassed, and quickly went for her room and closed the door behind her. Samara said to herself. "What can he be thinking of me peeking in on him? Get a hold of yourself, Samara, stop it!!!" Samara got in bed and pulled the covers

over her head but it didn't help, all she could see was that strong looking handsome man with muscles of steel!
Alan laid in his bed thinking about Samara. She sure was taking a good look at me he thought. She is such a lovely woman, he said to himself; never saw a woman that got my attention as she does. Alan rolled over and closed his eyes and all he could see was her standing there.

Chapter Thirteen

The next morning Alan got dressed, checked his guns and went out to see if the crew was getting ready to ride. Alan saw Sam, Greg, Ronnie and Phil sitting around the fire waiting for the coffee to finish. They all looked a little rough.

"What the hell happened?" Alan asked. "You guys look like you died and someone forgot to bury you."

"Didn't get a lot of sleep last night," Sam said, "A lot goin' on last night."

"I didn't get a hell of a lot a' sleep either." Phil added. "Way too much goin' on, that's fer' sure. Regular circus it was." Alan shook his head and said, "I was afraid of that. You men gotta' stop it with these gals. We need ta' get work done, not play men."

"Don't look at me boss." Phil answered. "I kept out the way as not to get broken bones."

"Just hold your boots on boss," Sam told Alan, "We get some coffee in us an' some eats an' we'll be ready to go."

Some of the girls came out to the fire and they didn't look to spunky either. Alan looked up to the sky as for looking for help, then told them,

"Better get yourselves together, and pretty damn quick. We got a lot to do today, and it's gonna' be a long hot day an' I need you guys to be ready an' on your best. I'm countin' on ya'."

"No problem Boss," Greg replied, "We'll be on top of it, don't worry. It wasn't as bad as your thinking and we feel better than we look."

“When we get time we’re going to make a bunk house for the men or put a wall in the middle of this one.”
“Don’t panic Boss, we’ll behave.” Ronnie said.
“We ride out in an hour men, get ready an’ make sure ya’ got enough water an’ your guns are loaded.” Alan told them and went back to the house for breakfast.
“Everyone gettin’ ready to go Alan?” Samara asked.
“Sort of Boss. It seems like it was a busy night in the bunk house last night. None of them look real ready.”
“Oh no, what happened?”
“Easier to ask what didn’t as far as I can tell ma’am.”
Samara raised her eyebrows and shook her head.
Molly brought out eggs, ham and hot biscuits.
“Made you lunch bags, Missy Halleck, to put in your saddle bags.”
“Thank you Molly, that was very nice of you.”
Molly grinned as she put the lunch bags on the table and told Samara to listen to Alan to keep her tail out of trouble. Samara’s eyes opened wide and said, “I’m the Boss, and I can handle my self, Molly!” Molly smiled and shook her head as she went to the kitchen and said, “You’re the Boss Missy, but you hired him to save your tail an’ the ranch, let him do his job.”
Samara went to stand to answer that remark but stopped.
“Don’t pay any attention to her Alan, she has too much opinion at times.” Alan just smiled.
They had their breakfast, gathered their belongings, and went out into the yard. Alan was shocked as all had their horses saddled, packed and were ready to ride.
“Looks like they’re all ready to go Alan.”

"Yes ma'am it looks that way, I wouldn't have thought they were gonna' make it from what I saw an hour ago. All right folks lets get to moving see ya' this evening. You know the plan. Be safe, be sure an' watch your backs."

They all mounted up and started riding to their assigned territories. Alan couldn't believe they bounced back from what he first saw in the morning.

Alan, Samara, Sabrina Zeagler, and Macy Allen, rode to the south end of the ranch. Sam and Greg Bledsoe with Kaycee Britt, Haley Hurst and Nicole Martin went to the west range. Ronnie Hall, Hennah Noel, Brooke Allen and Margaret Wiedenan headed north. The day was a little overcast with clouds but it was still going to be a warm one. At this time a couple of years ago the weather was stormy with rain causing floods in some areas of the ranch. Hopefully that wouldn't be a problem this year. The plan for all the groups were to ride into the Hayes Ranch property about a mile and gather any cattle with the H Bar brand and any that had a H Bar changed into the Circle H. As they pushed their cattle back any real Circle H cattle were to be singled out and back away from the Halleck's stock.

Things were going smoothly with Alan's group on the south end, gathering about forty cattle and pushing them to the Halleck range. All three groups were going to meet at a pre determined sector and then they would circle the herd and drive them deeper into their home range. After that they would go out daily to make sure they stayed there and continue to do so until the Law arrived.

Sam's group was just inside of the Halleck property when they saw several riders coming their way. Sam told all to be ready for trouble and he and Greg pulled back the thong from their pistols hammers. There were six of them.
"What ya' doin' folks?" One of them asked.
"Just gathering up our cattle," Sam replied, "Got any problem bout that?"
"No just as long as they all be yours."
"Just ours, we don't have any of your cattle, sorted 'em out."
"Mind if in we have a look-see, Fella?"
"Not at all, have a look." Sam told him.
"Howdy sis, when you goin' ta' be actin' as a lady again?" One of the Hayes riders asked.
"Don't pay him any mind," Haley said to Sam, "That's my brother Hunter."
"Least I ain't workin' for no crook, Hunter, got me an honest job."
"Least I'm a getting paid, sis."
"Yeah with dirty money Hunter, mom would be so proud of you!"
"Couple of those steers got Hayes brands on 'em boys," The leader of the Hayes men said, "cut 'em out."
"Hold it fella," Sam said, "Those brands are over our brand, been stolen an' redone over ours."
"That's a bunch of bull young fella, cut 'em out boys."
Greg rode his horse up to stop them. "Better move on boys." He told them.
The boss man grabbed for his gun and in a flash Greg pulled his Colt and shot him in the chest and the boss fell

off his horse dead. Suddenly the rest of the Hayes men had guns pointed at them. They froze.

"Better had move on back to you side," Sam said, "And take him with ya." Pointing at the man on the ground. Two of the Hayes men got off their horses and draped the dead man over his saddle and fastened him on.

"Hayes ain't gonna' like this," Hunter Hurst said, "Better get out while ya' can Sis." And they rode off.

"That was quick, Greg." Sam said.

"Just took my time, Sam, no need to hurry. You should see me when I'm serious." Sam shook his head.

Up on the north end Hennah Noel hollered to Ronnie Hall. "There a rider movin' fast."

Ronnie looked over and saw a big man wearing a black shirt and trousers with long white hair riding a big Dapple Grey. He came out of a wide crack in the canyon wall up ahead of Ronnie's group's position. He was moving fast, toward the Hayes property, seemingly paying them no mind at all. He had his horse at a full run. Ronnie wondered what was he doing up in the draw of the canyon wall, and who the hell was he?

The rest of the day went smoothly and the three groups pushed all the cattle to the meeting place. Sam told Alan what had happened and Ronnie told Alan of the rider he had seen.

"That sounds like Mark Hayes." Samara said.

"Yes it does," Alan answered, "What's he doing up in there by himself? Does he have cattle hidden back in there?"

"My Dad said he saw Mark up that way a couple of times and that's not far from where Daddy was found dead.' Samara said. "I've never been up in that part of the canyon. I've seen the wide crack but never went into it. Don't know if Dad ever did either, he never said."

"It's strange," Alan replied, "We'll have to check it out when we can, but lets move these cattle closer in and break for the night." They had gathered up a little over two hundred head of cows.

They rode back to the ranch and wiped down their horse and put their tack away. Windy met Alan and told him he sent the telegram and got the answer in about two hours. He told Alan that U.S. Marshal Buist was coming with another marshal and a Texas Ranger and they should be at the Halleck Ranch in two to three days. He gave the telegram to Alan and he in turn gave it to Samara. She was very happy about the news.

Alan and Samara got a bath and met in the dinning room. Samara poured a drink for the both of them and they sat at the table.

"Dinner's gonna' be bout twenty minutes Missy." Molly said.

Alan got up and went to the buffet where the bottle was to fix another drink for them both. He saw what appeared to be a large chunk of green glass. It was about six inches long, bigger than his thumb and was six sided.

"What's this? He asked.

"I don't know, Dad brought that home one day and set it there. I don't know where he got it or what it is, Alan." They had a good dinner, talked a while and turned in.

Chapter Fourteen

Alan got up at daybreak, got dressed and went out to see the hands. He had left orders for the herd to be watched in shifts through the night. Windy and Phil were making breakfast for the crew and Alan grabbed a cup of coffee. Four riders that had been on watch came riding in.

"All go OK?" Alan asked.

"Went well Boss, no trouble at all," Margaret answered, "We just got relieved and all was quiet all night."

"Good, glad to hear that," Alan replied, "But I expect trouble today, so be ready and be on the watch. Got a feeling it's the calm before the storm."

The whole crew agreed and said they would be alert.

Alan talked with Sam and went over the days assignments. Alan told Sam he expected Mark Hayes to do some retaliation over the shooting of one of his men. Sam told Alan that he, Greg and Ronnie were prepared for such a move from Mark.

"Breakfasts ready Alan." Molly hollered. Alan waved at Molly and told Sam to keep an eye on the herd and be on the look out. "We got it Boss." Sam told him and smacked him on the shoulder with a smile on his face.

Alan went to the house. Buster met him at the door and smelled his boots and snorted, wagging his tail.

"He likes you Alan," Samara said with a smile.

"I hope you will someday," Alan thought to himself as he walked to the table.

"We got a little over two hundred herd moved back," Alan told Samara, "We'll check in the heavy brush areas today an' see what we can move closer Boss."
"I'll ride with you again Alan."
"No need to ma'am. I'm going into Hays Town, with Sam and Phil to get some supplies. You can stay at the ranch today. I got the crews set up to ride today and the others will stay at the ranch to keep an eye on things."
"OK Alan, just be cautious."
"Will do Boss."
They finished breakfast and Alan was getting his things together for the ride into town when a horse could be heard riding up to the house. Samara looked out the window and was surprised at what she saw. It was Mark Hayes, alone.
"Alan, its Mark. Get into the bedroom so he can't see you. I don't know what he's up to, so be ready if I holler for you." Alan grabbed his thing and went to his bedroom but left the door ajar so he could hear well.
Mark Hayes walked to the door and all in the yard were watching him.
"Samara, you here?" He asked loudly.
"Yes I am, come in Mark, what can I do for you?"
Mark walked in he was a big man, towering over Samara. He glanced around the room. "You alone?" He asked.
"Just Molly working in the kitchen, that's all."
"Tell her to find something to do out side. I want to talk to you alone."
Samara asked Molly to go out side. As she left Mark closed the door.
"I don't need any trouble Mark."

"I'm not here to cause any this time, Missy. Beside you got enough trouble as it is."
"How is that?"
"You killed one of my men yesterday for starters."
"He asked for it Mark."
"I'm not here for a bunch of small talk, woman. Got a deal for you an' you might wanta' take it if you know what's good for you."
"And just what kinda' deal you got this time Mark?"
"I've tried to buy this place several times."
"It's not for sale!" Samara interrupted.
"I've offered you more than this place is worth, woman, much more, but this deal you better take."
Alan was listing through the crack of the door wondering where this was going and had his hand on his gun in case Mark got physical.
"Samara, I want you to marry me." Before he could say any more, Samara laughed and replied, "Marry you! Are you out of your mind Mark? I wouldn't marry you if you were the only man left alive on this earth."
"It's the only way you'll keep this ranch, lady. If you marry me you keep this ranch and my ranch is half yours too!"
"That's ridiculous, Mark. I wouldn't trust you to run this ranch and you'll find away to keep me from getting yours if anything happened to you. I know how you work, and my Dad would come out of his grave if I was foolish enough to do such a stupid thing."
"It's your only and last chance to do this peaceable lady."
"And if I don't?"

"I'll just take it my own way, Miss Halleck, better think it over. And you got no one to back up what was said here, but I will tell you this, I'll take this place real soon if you don't agree."

Samara chuckled to herself inside. If he only knew about Alan listening and the Marshal coming.

"By force, Mr. Hayes?"

"If need be Missy, you can bank on it."

"Mark Hayes, I think you should leave, and I mean now."

Mark laughed, "Or your gonna throw me out?"

Samara walked over to the corner grabbed her rifle and cocked it. "As a matter of fact I am Mark, now get out."

Mark was surprised, he didn't see that coming.

"You turning me down lady? You're dumber than I thought, and as pig headed as you're old man."

"Is that why you had him killed, Mark?"

"You might say that Missy, but there was more to it than that. And if you try to pin it on me it's your word against mine." Samara was red hot and her anger was at a boiling point. She pointed her rifle at Mark and pulled the trigger. The blast in the house was deafening, the bullet hitting the floor between Marks feet. Several of the hands ran up and opened the door in fear of what might have happened. Alan was looking out the door with his pistol in hand and could see Samara had all in control. Mark didn't see him, as he stepped back and said, "Should of killed me woman, big mistake. I'll take that as a no, but you ain't seen or heard the last of this. I'll be back." Mark turned and walked out, mounted his horse and rode off.

Alan came out and asked Samara if she was OK.

Samara dropped the rifle turned and grabbed Alan and hugged him.
"Sorta' wish Mark would come by more often," Alan thought to himself.
"I'm so glad you're here Alan, so glad. Did you hear everything?"
"Yes ma'am I did."
"He even admitted having Father killed."
"Yes, but he didn't say he did it himself Boss. I wish he had. Somehow we gotta' prove who did it by his orders."
"I've always known in my heart he had Dad killed."
Suddenly she realized she was holding Alan and her face went blush with embarrassment. "I'm sorry, I got caught up in my emotions, I'm sorry."
"Don't be," Alan told her, "Glad I could be here for you.."
"Thank you Alan, thank you for protecting me. And I'm glad you heard what he said."
"It's my job Boss, just doing my job."
"I'm glad I hired you Alan. You're the first man I have trusted in a long time."
"OK boss I got work to do, gotta' head for town, you stay at the ranch. There's no telling what he's got in mind."
Alan tipped his hat and went outside.

Chapter Fifteen

Alan got with Sam and Phil to get ready to go to town. He asked Greg to work on the round up and Ronnie to stay at the ranch with the others in case of trouble. Alan and Sam mounted up and Phil drove the buckboard. The road to Hays Town crossed the Hayes ranch property but it was considered a right away. They entered town and went to E.C. Hays store and tied off.

"Howdy young man, how are things working out for you?" Mr. Hays asked.

"Makin' progress Mr. Hays, getting things in order. Need to pick up some goods."

"Hope I can fill your needs son."

Alan gave Mr. Hays a list and he looked it over.

"Looks like I got what you need fella', wanta' wait for it?"

"Yes Sir, but I'm gonna' go to the Black Steer an' talk to Don for a minute or two. Phil here will help you load it."

Alan and Sam walked to the Black Steer Saloon. Sam asked Alan what had happened at the house and Alan gave the short version.

Don saw them come in and wiped the bar for them.

"Have a drink?" He asked.

"No I just want to ask you some questions and maybe get some pointers." Alan Replied.

"Having any trouble?"

"Not too much Don. Had a run in with some of Hayes boys yesterday."

"I heard about that," Don said, "Words all over town. Does Mark know your working for the Halleck woman yet?"

"No not yet but I think it's about time he did."
"Be careful around him Alan, he's quick tempered and fast to use a gun, an' he's mighty quick with them too."
"I'll keep an' eye out. Let me ask you if you've ever seen anything like this." Alan said, pulling out the green glass object, laying it on the bar.
Don looked at it and said, "As a matter of fact, I think I saw that piece before. Ole Man Halleck brought it in some time back an' showed it to me."
"Is it some sort of glass?"
"Mighty expensive glass, my friend," Don said, 'It's Topaz, worth more than gold fella."
"Did Mr. Halleck tell you where he found it?"
"No he wouldn't tell me where he found it, but I will tell you this. Mark Hayes brought one in not to long after Ole Man Halleck was killed. Wasn't as big as that one but it sure was pretty though."
"Did he say how or where he got it?" Alan asked.
"He wouldn't say, but let me show you something. Terri can I see ya' for a minute?"
Terri came over next to Don asking what he needed.
"Show Mr. Holt your necklace hun." Terry had a gold chain around her neck and she held it out with a stone like Alan brought in about the size of a nickel.
"Hayes brought that in one day and traded to me for a couple drinks." Don told Alan. "That was a hell of a deal pal."
Alan looked at the stone and then at Sam. "Are you thinking what I'm thinking Sam?"
"I think I am, Alan."

“Don’t say anything about this, Sam. But we need to check out that crack in the canyon wall.”
“I think your right, Alan, just might be something there. Samara’s dad was killed near there and Mark has been seen in that area several times.”
“First Sam we gotta’ get the ranch under control, then we can check it out. Just keep it to your self for now though.”
“Will do buddy.”
Alan and Sam walked back to Mr. Hay’s store. Phil and Mr. Hay’s handyman had the wagon loaded and ready to travel.. Alan thanked Mr. Hays and paid him for the supplies. Alan and Sam mounted up for the ride to the ranch and met two of Mark’s men riding into town. One of the riders was Haley’s brother Hunter. They stopped in the middle of the street blocking Alan, Sam and Phil driving the wagon.
“Ain’t you one of the men that killed Smitty?” Hunter asked, looking at Sam.
“Don’t know any Smitty.” Sam replied.
“You were there when he got shot, cowboy. If Mark was here he kill ya’. An you, the other one,” Hunter said looking at Alan, “Ain’t you the drifter that stopped at the Hayes ranch askin’ for a job?”
“Might have been,” Alan replied, “But I got a job now.”
“Workin’ for that Halleck woman?” Hunter asked.
“Yeah you might say that, I’m the new ranch boss.” Alan replied.
‘Well cowboy, you ain’t too bright,” Hunter said with a grin, “Cause ya’ll be dead real soon.” He looked at the man with him and they both laughed and rode into town.

“OK boys lets get moving.” Alan said and they stared on for the ranch.
As they were unloading the supplies Samara came out to meet them.
“Have any trouble, Alan?”
“No ma’am, did all go well here?”
“Yes it was quiet, that worries me a little.”
“Yes, me too boss. Let’s hope it stays quiet until the Marshall get’s here to put an’ end to this crazy man’s actions. I was told in town by Haley’s brother we will all be dead in a couple of days.”
“I don’t like that kind of talk Alan.”
“I don’t either boss. We better be ready for his next move.”
‘Don’t worry you two,” Sam said, “We’ll be ready.” Sam gave a thumbs up sign. Alan patted him on the back and told him again how glad he was to have him and his boys on the ranch. “You’d do the same for me Alan.”
“Get washed up and come for a drink before dinner,” Samara told Alan, “Windy killed an’ elk today, that should be real good.”
Alan tipped his hat and went to clean up. The hot bath felt real good. He got dressed and walked to the house. Samara met him with a tall drink. They went sat down in the living room and talked for a while. Greg came up on the porch.
“Can I see ya’ boss?” He asked.
“Come in Greg,” Samara told him. What’s up?”
“As I was riding the north range today I saw Mark Hayes come out of the canyon, he didn’t see me. He was riding hard an’ fast.” Samara and Alan looked at each other puzzled.

Chapter Sixteen

Samara and Alan had a good diner made by Molly then went out on the porch to sit in the rockers. Buster came up, sniffed Alan, snorted and went to lay down. They finally decided to hit the beds and Samara wished Alan a good night he responded the same to her.

Samara went straight to her room not daring to take a peak in Alan's room. She thought that was so embarrassing. They both fell asleep quickly.

"OK boys, you know what to do," Mark told his men, "I'll ride into town an' get a couple of drinks. That way they can't say I did it. Now remember, this time I don't want anyone hurt, just scare the hell out of them. Maybe they'll get the idea."

All the men agreed and went out to mount up and head for the Halleck Ranch. Mark headed for town. He had a smile on his face; he thought this was a good plan.

Alan had been asleep about two hours. He had told Sam to place sentry's to watch for trouble so he felt comfortable. All of a sudden he was awakened by gun fire. A lot of gun fire. He jumped up, grabbed his rifle and looked out the window. Samara was right behind him.

"What's going on? She asked

'Don't really know. The only people I see out there is our people. Get away from the window."

It was a constant volley of fire and who ever was doing the shooting were well hidden. Suddenly shots came through the front windows showering glass everywhere. Alan pushed Samara to the floor.

"I can't get a shot," Alan said, "Can't see 'em."

It went on for about ten minutes then as suddenly as it started, it stopped. Sam could hear horses running and took a couple of shots in that direction. He thought he heard someone yell as if being hit but he couldn't really tell for sure.

Everyone checked to see if anyone was hurt, but there weren't any casualties. They had knocked out all the windows in the front of the house and the bunk house. They shot several holes in the water tower and it was leaking a lot of water.

"That tank will be empty by morning," Alan told Samara, "Well have to fix it first thing in the morning."

They went out side to check on everyone.

"Couldn't see 'em boss," Sam said, "But I think I hit one. Don't know for sure though."

"OK everyone lets get back to bed. We'll check the damage in the morning." Alan said, and he and Samara went back to the house. This time Alan had a hard time going to sleep. He laid there for a while wondering who was responsible, but he had a good idea.

His bedroom door opened and Samara came in wearing her nightgown covered by her robe.

"I sorry Alan, but my windows have been shot out and I don't feel safe."

"That's OK boss, I'll sleep on the floor."

"You afraid I'm gonna' hurt you Alan? You stay on your side an' I'll stay on mine." Alan was hoping she wouldn't.

The next morning Allan woke and she was already gone. Alan got with Sam to assess the damage. Phil Burd joined them. "I'm gonna' be busy for a day or so." Phil said.
"We'll have to go to town an' get some window glass Phil, can you cut it to fit."
"Ole man Hays can cut it if we give him the size. Gonna' cost some money Alan. Glass is expensive around here."
Windy had cut some plugs to stop the leaks in the water tower and had put them in. They hung blankets in the bunkhouse window frames. The night crews came in and the day crews went out to cover the herd. The night crew said they saw several riders moving fast and hard, headin' west. Alan didn't think that was a coincidence.
Alan, Sam and Ronnie Hall road into town to get the glass. Mr. Hays looked over the list and told them it would take several days to get that much glass. "I got some, but not enough for you to finish. You want me to cut what I have?"
"Yes Mr. Hays, I'll send Phil in to pick it up."
Alan, Sam and Ronnie went to the Black Steer Saloon to look around. "How's it going?" Don asked.
"Had a little excitement last nigh Don." Alan told him what had happened and said he was going to the sheriff and tell him about it. "Wont do ya' no good my man," Don said, "He wont do nothing."
Sam looked over at a table and saw one of Marks men wearing a sling.
"What happened to you fella?"
"Shot my self cleaning my gun."
"That's a shame," Sam replied, "Were ya' cleaning your gun at the Halleck Ranch last night?"

The cow hand stood up with his hand resting on his gun. "You accusing me of having a hand it that?" He said to Sam.

"I don't have too," Sam replied, "You just told me ya' did. Nobody in town has heard about it yet. Now you just sit back down or I'll fix your other shoulder."

The man sat down.

They walked over to the sheriff's office and told the sheriff what had happened the night before.

"See who done it?" The sheriff asked.

"No sir we couldn't see 'em." Alan told him.

"Well you get me something to work on an' I'll look into it for ya'."

Alan and his boys just shook their heads and walked out.

"That man with a sling, tell the sheriff, that's the guy I hit Alan, he all but told us he was there."

Alan turned back into the sheriff's office,.and told him about the man in the sling.

"I'll look into it fella'. He said to Alan.

"Don't hold your breath."

Alan's and his group rode back to the ranch. On the way they met several of Mark's men riding into town. They all just tipped their hats to each other and rode on.

They got back to the ranch and Windy met them.

"We'd better get busy, Boss." He said to Alan, "Cow are calving heavy an' little ones are all over the place."

"OK Windy we'll start tomorrow morning." Alan said. "We'll rope 'em brand out there." Windy agreed and went on to tell the others. Alan took his saddle off Buddy and wiped him down and then he reached into his pocket and

gave Buddy a piece of rock candy he had picked up at Hays's store. Buddy liked that and nudged for more.
"That's enough for today ole pal. Don't want to ruin yer' teeth. Let me give ya' a mite of oats to chew on. Better for them teeth." Alan walked him to the corral and gave him a bit of oaks. Buddy looked disappointed, but he started nibbling on it as Alan walked to the house. When he got there Samara was sitting in the living area reading.
"Hi Alan, all go well in town?"
"Yeah Boss, gonna have ta' wait a couple of day's for all the glass, but Phil is going to get what Mr. Hays has, so at least we can get started. We'll get your bedroom first and what we can get done in the front off the house."
"You afraid I'm gonna hog your bed to long?" Samara said with a sheepish grin.
"No ma'am, I'll share."
Alan told her about Sam confronting the wounded cow hand and what the sheriff told him. He also said they met some of Hayes men, but nothing became of it. He also told her what Windy told him about calves dropping and they would start branding in the morning.
"Well I don't look forward to hearing much from the sheriff Alan. He's one of Hayes's men, after all, Hayes is the man that made him sheriff. I figured the cattle would be dropping heavy soon. I'll help if you need me."
"I think we we'll be OK boss, no need for you to be in the heat all day."
"Ain't my first Alan, done it many times with Dad. Why don't you clean up an' come back for a drink before dinner, that's what I'm gonna' do. See ya' in a bit."

Alan went back to wash up and when he went to the wash hours there was only one tub open and it was in the middle of the five. The other tubs were being used by four of the gal's. Alan took a deep breath, grabbed his towel and got in the tub with his under shorts still on.
"Smatter Boss, fraid' we'll see sometin'?" Margaret asked.
Alan shook his head and went on about washing up. He went back the house and was met by Samara all gussied up with a drink in her hand.
"You are lovely Boss, I mean lovely."
"Glad you think so Alan, never thought about it much myself." She said with a twinkle in her eye. Alan smiled and told her about what happened in the wash house. Samara laughed.
"Tell ya' what, Alan, why don't you use the tub here in the house? My Dad did."
"Well Boss, I…."
"Just do it, more private for you and it'll give the gal's other things to think about."
"Yeah, like Sam, Greg and Ronnie!" Alan replied and Samara laughed. She looked even lovelier when she smiled.
They had a nice meal from the elk Windy had gotten. Alan asked where she got the ice for the drinks each night.
"Daddy dug a deep ice cellar built in back of the house. He had it double cedar lined with sawdust and straw inside the planks. We go out in the spring and get ice from the mountains and fill it up. Lasts all summer."
They sat and talked on the porch and went on to bed. Alan laid there, my lord she smelled good. He slid his hand toward Samara, "Night Alan." His hand retreated slowly.

Chapter Seventeen

The next morning, after breakfast, the day crew saddled up followed by the buckboard loaded with the portable forge and the branding irons, and pulled out to meet the herd. Sam stayed at the ranch with the night crew to keep an eye on things. Ronnie and Greg went with Alan and the branding crew. Phil Burd drove the chuck wagon to make a lunch and carry water for the crew. Didn't take long before they were in full swing, roping an' branding. Alan was impressed how well the gal's could rope, they were really good. They roped the calves, threw down and pig tied them. As soon as they were branded the gal's let 'em go bawling to their moms. The group was making good time. Hennah Noel looked back and said, "Would ya' look at that we just did that bunch over there and some cows are laying to drop a calf."

"We'll get them tomorrow," Sabrina told her, "Let 'em get a little strength first." And they went after the cows ahead. It was getting hot and Phil was handing out water, and filling canteens hand over fist. By noon they probably had branded over two hundred calves.

Alan was impressed how well and hard these gal's were working. Greg and Ronnie were riding shotgun so to speak, keeping an eye out for trouble but so far it was going smooth. They broke for a lunch break and the temperature was over a hundred degrees. Windy Lee was acting as wrangler keeping the fresh horses ready to exchange. With this heat the horses were worn out in four hours, with lather on them like soap suds. The only thing Phil made hot was coffee. One thing about a cowboy, no matter how hot it was they wanted their coffee even if it was cold.

Mark Hayes called his men together for a meeting.
"Men we gotta' make our move, and quick. I'm tiered of that woman running me around. I've tried to make her a peaceful deal several times, but she's to bull headed, like her ole' man was. She need's to have an accident, and soon. I don't care how you get it done, but get it done. If you can't make it look an accident, hide the body so no one knows or can prove how it happened. Maybe everyone will think she just ran off."
"Well boss we got a problem," Hunter Hurst said, "Member that guy that stopped at the ranch lookin' for a job? Well he's working for that Halleck woman. Runnin' the place he is. And he's got three men he's brought in with him. One of them is the guy that killed Smitty. He is deadly fast with a gun."
"Don't make no difference how many men he's got or how fast they are, we got better or I'm paying money to a bunch of lackeys. Now let's get this over with. I'm tired of foolin' around. So let's get to work, men, and I mean now!" They all tipped their hats at Mark and went out to mount up.

Around three o'clock Sam was sitting in the shade of the bunkhouse rolling a smoke and he saw a cloud of dust in the distance. He went inside the bunkhouse and got a pair of binoculars to have a better look. It was about ten or so riders coming fast. He alerted the gal's to grab their rifles and hide out of sight. He then ran to the house to warn

Samara, and she grabbed her rifle and stood by the door. It was some of Marks men, and they charge right though the front gate, pistols drawn.
"Let 'em get close an' let 'em have it if they start shooting." Sam ordered.
Sure enough Mark's men rode in and opened up, shooting in all directions.
"Give it to 'em." Sam hollered and all hell broke loose. Half of Mark's men hit the dirt and didn't move. The rest turned tail and ran off. One of the gals hollered at Sam.
"Sam, behind you!"
Sam turned and saw three men coming hard at a run for the ranch. "Get ready." Sam shouted, and he cocked his rifle. The three men stopped about a hundred yards off and shouted; "U. S. Marshal, wish to come in."
"Hold your fire," Sam told his group, "It's the Marshal we've been waiting for." And he waved to the three men to come in. They came into the yard and one of the said; "I'm U. S. Marshal Ed Buist," and pointed at the other two, "This is Marshal Alex Schuring and Bruce McHenry, Texas Ranger at your service." He looked in the yard and saw five bodies lying on the ranch grounds. "Have some trouble? We heard the gun fire as we were riding in and came to help, but looks to me you handled it."
"It was some of Mark Hayes's men. Been having trouble with them, a lot lately." Sam told Ed.
"Well we're here to put an end to this, fella.' Understand he's rustling cattle, threatening bodily harm, and a possible murder charge is to be looked into." Ed replied.
Samara came out to meet the lawmen.

“So glad you’re here Marshal. It will be glad to put an end to all the threats and bullying from Mark Hayes. He thinks he owns this country.”

“Well ma’am we are here to help you, and put an end to all this trouble he’s causing,” Marshal Ed told her, “We’re gonna’ get on it first thing tomorrow morning.”

Sam told the crew to put the bodies on their horses and tie them down, and then chase the horses off.

“They’ll go on back to the Hayes ranch and he can bury his men.” Sam told them.

“Mind if we freshen up? It’s been a long dusty, hot ride.” Marshall Buist asked.

“Help your self,” Samara told them, “There’s hot tub in the bunk house. When you’re finished, come on to the house and have a drink.”

Ed, Alex and Bruce thanked Samara and went to put up their horses before washing up. Samara thank Sam for making sure all was ready for the attack from Mark Hayes’s men.

“No problem Boss, glad I saw them coming.”

“Sam, tell Alan when he gets in that the law made it. I’m sure that will make him feel better.” Sam tipped his hat and went on to see if he could help the marshal’s and the ranger.

Chapter Eighteen

Mark Hayes was mad as hell when he found out what happened at the Halleck ranch and called every available hand to his house for a meeting.
"What the hell were you nitwits thinking? I said to make it look like an accident, or ambush and hide the body. But you went charging in there like a bunch of rouge Injun's. I'm paying you idiot's good wages to do an important job and all you're doing is stinking it up. I ain't gonna' put up with this nonsense. You're gonna do it right or I'll find somebody that can. Now do you understand what I just said?"
All the hands said they would.
"Good, now you half ass idiots start listening to and do what I ask or I'm gonna start shooting and it wont be at the Halleck's men. Now get out of here and wait for my orders!"
They all cleared the house quickly. Mark started to walk around the living room thinking how he was going to kill that Halleck woman. He was disgusted. He had to come up with a plan and quick. He had no idea what was coming in the morning. Things were going to get intrusting.

Alan rode in with the branding crew and dismounted. They had a long hard, hot, dusty day and were worn out. Sam told him of the lawmen arriving and what had happened earlier.
"Glad their here Sam, and I'm glad you handled the Hayes men without any loss or harm to ours."

"Glad to do it Alan. I was also glad I saw them coming so we could get set up and surprise them. You should have seen their faces. I think they thought the ranch was nearly empty, they didn't expect what they got. Here, I'll take care of Buddy for ya', you go get freshened up."

"Thanks Sam. Good job. I'm gonna take your advice."

Alan walked up the house and told Samara how it went in the field.

"Got most of the calves done finished today, only a few stragglers left to do boss."

"Good Alan your doing a great job. I'm glad I have you and your men to help. Would you like a drink?"

"Let me get my bath and change first, then I'll join ya' so you can fill me in on what happened here today."

"OK Alan, I'll have your drink ready when you're done. I'm going to have the marshal's and the ranger for dinner tonight and I want you to ask Sam, Ronnie and Greg to join us also, if you will."

Alan smiled, told Samara how nice she looked and went to clean up.

Samara watched him walk away and thought she finally met a man besides Phil and Windy she could trust. And a good looking man at that!

Alan took a bath and shaved then came out to join Samara. They sat in the living room and had a nice cool drink of bourbon. Samara told him all about the attack, and how well Sam had handled it.

"Glad he was here to protect you and the help," Alan said, "I've known Sam for several years and he gives his best."

“He did at that Alan, he really handled it well. Those Hayes men didn’t know what hit them.”
“I’m gonna’ quick run out and tell Sam to come and bring Ronnie and Greg. I’ll be right back.” Alan went out and met Ed, Bruce and Alex coming to the house.
“You must be Alan,” Marshal Buist said, “Got here as fast as we could. Hope we can get this takin’ care of quickly for you. We have some more rustling and Apache trouble we gotta’ look into further south when we are done here. It seems like it doesn’t get any better now ‘a days and we don’t have the man power we need to do the job”
“This Mark Hayes has been makin’ trouble for this ranch for some time now marshal and he is suspected of having Samara’s father killed also.”
“Well my man we gotta prove that first. Got any witnesses?”
“Just speculation right now, sir, no one has the nerve to speak out for fear of their lives, Mark controls this part of the country, even the so called sheriff.”
“I checked up on that sheriff also, Alan, and he’s not registered with the state of Texas as a sheriff, so I’ll handle that too!” Ed answered.
“I’ll see you at the house,” Alan replied, “Gotta to tell a couple more to join us.” They all shook hands and Alan went to see Sam and tell him about Samaras plans for the evening and to bring Greg and Ronnie.
When everyone arrived Samara asked them to enjoy a drink. When Alan introduced Greg and Ronnie to Marshall Buist he asked, “Do I know you two fellows, you both look familiar for some reason?”

"Spent some time in Texas, Kansas and Oklahoma, punchin' cows off 'an on," Greg answered, "Might of seen us there."
Ed looked at him and asked, "How about Missouri or Iowa?'
"Can't say we were." Ronnie answered.
Ed nodded his head and asked to get done to business.
They all gathered around the table to discus the problems at hand. Marshal Buist, told them his plan was, that he, Marshall Alex Schuring, Ranger Bruce McHenry, and Alan would ride over to the Hayes Ranch and arrest Mark Hayes on cattle rustling. Then they would ride into Hays Town and confront the acting sheriff. "Do they have a jail in Hays Town?" Marshal Ed Buist asked.
"Sort of," Alan answered, "Not much of a jail, but it does have a cell in it."
"Good," Ed replied, "We can hold Hayes there while we get all the information we can against him, and see what we can determine about the murder of this lady's father."
"You might want to see what you can find out about his so called buying the Wyler Ranch, and Mr. Wyler's robbery and death." Samara added.
"This might take more time than I figured," Ed said, "I forgot about that. I gotta' get busy."
Molly had prepared a fine roast goose dinner with all the fixings. They continued discussing the task at hand as they ate dinner. When dinner was over Marshal Buist told them he would lay out his plans in the morning. He thanked Samara for the great meal, and then they all adjourned for the evening.

Chapter Nineteen

In the morning, Alan and Samara were up before dawn. Molly was making breakfast and asked if the lawmen were going to join in. Alan went out and found Ed, Alex and Bruce were having the morning meal with Sam, Ronnie, Greg, Phil and Windy. Alan went back and told Molly.

"Alan, I want you to be careful today," Samara said, "Be on your guard. I'll be so glad when this is over."

"You worrying about me Boss?"

"Alan, yes I worry about all of you. I don't want to see anyone hurt."

"Oh, I thought you were fretting over me boss."

"Alan don't be silly. You're a big help and I appreciate what you're doing to help. That's all." But inside Samara was worried. Alan is a fine looking strong man, and he's on her mind a lot lately.

Alan was thinking he would love the chance to be near Samara. But then again, he was just one of the hired help, but maybe, just maybe!

Marshall Buist knocked on the door. Samara told him, "Come in Marshall, please come in."

"OK folks," he told them, "Here's my plan of action. I'll take Alan, Bruce and Alex with me to the Hayes ranch. We'll look around and check for Halleck cattle in his corrals. We then can arrest on rustling charges and hold him till' we can get the necessary info on the murder charges. I want Ronnie and Greg to go to Hays Town."

Marshall Ed Buist told Ronnie and Greg he would deputize them to hold the sheriffs office in Hayes town, and to arrest the acting fake sheriff. They both smiled at that comment. Ed gave them a letter to show they were territorial U.S. Marshalls under his command.

"OK Ronnie and Greg, you head for town, take care of business and wait for us to get up with you," Marshall Ed said, "Make sure all in town knows your handling the law. The rest of us are heading for the Hayes Ranch. OK, lets get moving."

Alan told Samara all was going to just fine and not to worry. Samara suddenly gave his a hug and told him to be careful. Alan smiled and turned to leave.

"Please take care!" Samara said as he walked out.

"I'll be fine Boss." Maybe she is takin' a shine to me, he thought to him self. Made him feel good.

They all mounted up and started on their missions. Not to far out Marshall Ed said to Alan, "Those two boys Ronnie and Greg, I figured out who they are. They have been in quiet a few gun fights and both are very quick. Almost as quick as Chuck Shoemaker. I just hope they don't try him, might not turn out to well."

"Why did you make them deputies if they're gun fighters?"

"All their fights have been in self defense or protecting themselves. No charges pending. But being quick and alert they'll make good lawmen, if they keep their nose's clean" Ed replied.

They rode on and crossed the boundary line between the two ranches and after several miles they saw some drovers pushing about fifty head of cattle.

"Let's check them." Marshal Buist said, and they rode toward them. When they caught up with the bunch one of the drovers asked, "What ya' doin?"
"Wanta' check your cattle boys, U.S. Marshal." Ed told them and showed his badge. One of the drovers sprinted off in a hurry. The head man asked, "What for? We ain't breakin' no law, just moving cattle to the holding corral."
"Well let's have a look-see anyway," Ranger McHenry said, "Have a look, Mr. Holt." Alan circled the herd to look them over. "Eight on 'em are Halleck cattle, Marshal Buist."
"OK cut 'em out," Ed ordered, and pointed to the Hayes men, "You two push 'em back to the Halleck line unless you want to be arrested for rustling."
The man who seemed to be in charge of the group, said, "We didn't notice they weren't ours, just a mistake. Go a head you two, push 'em back. Don't wanta' break no laws."
"Why did your other man run off?" Ed asked.
"Don't rightly know marshal. Musta' had to relieve his self, I guess."
Marshal Buist just smiled, and said, "Maybe he knew better, now get a movin'."
The Hayes men started pushing the cattle on.
"No hard feeling, marshal, just didn't notice those Halleck cows."
"I wonder what we'll find at the ranch corral?" Alan said to Marshal Buist.
They started following Mark's men to the ranch.

Chapter Twenty

Greg and Ronnie rode into Hayes Town and tied off in front of the sheriff's office and walked in. There was a man sitting in a chair reading a newspaper.
"You the sheriff?" Greg asked.
"No I'm just a sittin' here my friend."
"Where can we find the sheriff?" Ronnie asked.
"Most likely at the Black Steer Saloon, havin', a lunch break, I spose'."
Greg and Ronnie turned and started for the Black Steer. They walked through the batwing doors and saw several men sitting at the tables eating lunch. A few men were at the bar having a shot or two of whisky. Gregg and Ronnie walked up to the bar and were met by Don Volsch, the owner.
"What ya' have boys?" Don asked.
"The sheriff in here?" Greg asked.
"Well yes he is," Don said nodding his head to the left, "Sittin' at the table next to the piano."
"First let me show you this." Greg said as he pulled out the letter written by Marshal Buist showing their authority to take over as the new law in town. Don read the letter and smiled, and said. "Gotta' see this, can't wait."
Greg and Ronnie walked over to table where the so called sheriff was sitting and stood there waiting to be noticed.
"Can I help you boys?"
"Who are you?" Ronnie asked.
"I'm Wes Blair, the sheriff here a bout's. What can I do for ya'?

"Stand up 'an drop your gun belt," Greg told him, "Your under arrest for impersonating a officer of the law." The saloon went silent and Ronnie turned to cover Greg's back.
"What's the meaning of this? You boys crazy?"
Greg showed the letter to Wes Blair, he looked at it and his face went blank. "This is nonsense, I ain't gonna do no such thing."
"Drop your belt or I'll do it for you."
The sheriff quickly stood up and went for his gun. There was a deafening blast and Wes Blair went back over his chair, landing on the floor dead. Now the saloon was so quiet you could hear fly land on a table cloth.
"Anyone else?" Ronnie asked. No one moved.
Don Volsch asked a couple of men to drag Wes out the doors. "He's makin' a mess of my floor." Two men grabbed Blair's body by the arms and pulled him outside.
"OK folk's, it's all over," Greg said, "There's gonna' be law 'an order in Hays Town from now on. Tell 'em mister bar keep."
Don made the notice of the contents of the letter he saw. A lot of men shook their heads and started talking in small groups.
"Well Ronnie, we don't have to worry about putting him in the lockup."
"No Greg looks like he wanted to move on to other things."
They shook hands and Greg said. "OK folks, this town is gonna' get a clean up. If you can't abide by the law, time to move on. Hayes isn't runnin' things here anymore. If you

can abide by the law and be peaceable you're welcome to stay, other wise, clear out."

Several of the men went up to Greg and Ronnie and shook their hands and told them it was about time for things to change.

Greg and Ronnie went to the sheriff's office and started to go through the paper o and in the desk looking for clues. The man sitting in the chair asked, "Find the sheriff?"

"Yes you're looking at 'em, Ronnie answered, "So what do you do around here?"

"Mostly run errands for Wes."

"Well you can run errands for us now."

The man looked like he didn't know what to do, what's happening, he thought. Greg explained to him what had taken place and that he and Ronnie were now in charge.

"OK with me," the man answered, "We needed a change, the way I see it. Let me know if you be needin' sometin'." He got up and left the office.

"Well Ronnie, I'll take the first walk around town. See you in a bit." Greg adjusted his gun belt and went into the street. The undertaker was loading Blair's body with the help of some of the cowmen on the street. They all tipped their hats at Greg. This is gonna be a blast, Greg thought.

Alan, Marshal Buist and the other two law men, Alex and Bruce rode into the Hayes ranch and went straight to the large corral filled with cattle ready to go to market. As they were glancing over the cattle a big burly cow hand came to them.

"What ya' doin' fellas'?" He asked.

"Lookin' at the cattle, my friend." Marshall Buist answered.

"Wantin' to buy some cows?" The ranch hand said.

"Twenty two dollars a head, good price I say."

"Maybe so, but looks to me you got a lot of cattle with different brands on 'em."

"We bought 'em, time been hard and some ranches sellin', you ain't be sayin' we rustled them cows, are ya."

Ed pulled back his jacket and showed his badge. "As a matter of fact I am saying just that. We caught some of your men heading Halleck cattle this way this morning. Now you better do some talkin' or you're up to your tail in big trouble."

"I ain't sayin' nothing. You talk to the boss. I do what I get paid for, that's all."

"You getting paid to rustle?" With that the man walked for the main house.

"OK men," Ed said , "Let's do our job and take Mark Hayes in." With that they walked to front on the house.

Mark walked out on the porch. Ed was surprised when he saw this big, long white haired man with two ivory handled Colt's strapped low on his hips. Ed eased over to Alan and said, "Big boy, mighty big."

"What you lookin' for?" Mark asked.

"We're looking for you Mr. Hayes, your under arrest for cattle stealing, among other things. Now unbuckle your gun belt, real careful like."

Mark reached over and rang the bell hanging from the porch pillar. Suddenly the law men had twenty or more guns pointing at them.

"I don't know who you are," Mark said, "But I'm giving you just two minutes to get off my place or your gonna' get carried off."
"Your talking to a U.S. Marshal," Ed replied, "Now tell your men to lower their guns."
"This ain't the U.S., Mark answered, "This is Texas, now get moving while you still can."
"Texas belongs to the U.S. Mr. Hayes, now drop your guns." With that Mark pulled both Colt's out, pointed them at Ed, and cocked them.
"This is my land and I'm tellin' ya' to get off, now!"
Alex looked at Bruce, them Ed and Alan, "Ed we don't stand a chance. We're out numbered four to one. I think we need ta' ride out and regroup."
"I think he's right Marshal." Alan agreed.
"OK Mr. Hayes," Ed Buist said, "We'll meet another day."
"Yeh, on boot hill, Mr. lawman. Now get off my land, I'm loosing patience."
Ed turned to the men , "OK boys, let's ride. Head for town."
They rode into town and met Greg and Ronnie. Greg told Ed that the sheriff wasn't a problem anymore.
"That's a shame we could have got some valuable info outa' him." Marshall Ed said.
"Couldn't help it Mr. Ed, he pulled on me, had ta' do it sir."
"That's right sir," Ronnie added, "He went for his gun, he had no choice."
"OK," Marshal Buist replied. "Let's get a room, wash up, and get a meal. Tomorrow morning I'll deputize the whole

town if I have too. I gonna' get Mark Hayes, you can bet on it."

"He certainly has no regard for the law." Marshal Alex added.

"Not at all," Ranger McHenry added, "He's just plain poison."

They went to the Black Steer Saloon and saw Terry Volsch, Don's wife, about a room. She told them there was hot water in the bath house and to let her know about dinner. Greg and Ronnie said they would meet the others for dinner and were going to stay at the sheriff's office as there were two bunks there in a side room.

Ed, Alan, Alex and Bruce went to the rooms to get ready for their baths. Each room had accommodations for two each. Alan and Ed shared one and Alex and Bruce the other.

After washing up, they all met at a table with Greg and Ronnie joining them. They had a drink and ordered dinner. They discussed their plans for the next day.

"I'm gonna' get this damn fool." Ed Buist told them. "His luck is about to turn. We're gonna need a lot of men."

"Do you think the town's folk will help?" Alan asked.

"They better if they want to live in freedom again." Ed replied.

"You'll get some help," Don Volsch, the saloon owner said, "Most around here have been afraid of Mark Hayes, but with you here I think most will wanta' help."

Chapter Twenty One

Just before dark two riders rode into the Halleck Ranch yard and one said, "I want to see my sister."

Margaret Wiedenan and Hennah Noel came out of the bunkhouse, with pistols in hand, and asked, "Who's your sister?"

" Haley, Haley Hurst."

Sam saw them ride in and started to walk over their way.

"What do you want?" Sam asked.

"I want to talk to my sister."

By that time a lot of the crew in the bunkhouse came in the yard and his sister Haley asked, "What do you want Hunter?"

"I want you to get out of here sis. Marks coming and he's gonna' wipe this place off the map. I don't want you to be hurt."

"I ain't gonna get hurt Hunter. I've got a lot of friends here to take care of me."

"Better move on fellas'." Sam told the two riders.

"I ain't going without my sis."

"I said move on, and now."

The rider on Hunter's right side reached for his pistol and Margaret and Hennah opened up on him, knocking him to the ground. Hunter reached for his pistol and as he did his horse lurched sideways and when Sam fired, instead of hitting him in the chest the bullet cut a slash across Hunters chest like a ragged saber slash. Hunter grabbed his chest and fell to the ground in terrible pain, bleeding like a slaughtered hog.

Haley Hunter screamed; "Stop, stop, please stop, that's my brother." And she ran to him and cradled him in her arms, and hollered, "We need a doctor, somebody, I need help for my brother."
"Get Sabrina here she's studying to be a doctor." Someone said. "She's the best we can do at this point."
Sabrina came running to Hunter and looked at the wound. "Oh good heavens," She said, "This is serious, very serious, get him to the bunkhouse. I'll need plenty of hot water, clean bandages and lots of silk thread and a needle."
They carried Hunter into the bunk house and put him on a bunk. By this time he was passed out and Haley was crying. Sam came in and told Haley he was sorry, but Hunter was going to pull on him.
"I know, if his horse hadn't shifted, you would have killed him." Haley said.
"Sorry Haley," Sam answered, "It was him or me."
"I know Sam, you had no choice."
Hunter opened his eyes and reached his hand to Haley's face but his arm fell and his eyes closed.
"Is he dead?" Haley asked Sabrina.
"No he's passed out, he's in shock," Sabrina answered, "Now yall' get back and let me work on him and keep me in hot water."

In the morning Marshal Ed Buist asked Don to tell all that came in there would be a town meeting at nine o'clock and for him to suggest for all to attend. Don agreed.
Ed, Alan, Bruce, Alex, Greg and Ronnie sat at a table and Terri took their order for breakfast and poured coffee. Ed

started discussing his plans for taking the Hayes ranch with his group.

"Here's the way I see it, men. Mark Hayes is gonna' expect us to hit him today. He knows we are U.S. Marshall's and a Texas Ranger. He's gotta' take us out and hide any evidence that we were ever here and take back his town. I'm gonna' send a telegram to headquarters this morning so they will know we are here and if they don't hear from us by tomorrow evening to send it the Calvary. I'll tell headquarters he's guilty of rustling cattle and a possible two murder charges. He'll be ready an' waitin' for us so we're gonna' fool him boys. After we get all we can to join us, we'll ride back to the Halleck ranch. He'll think we gave up."

"Do you think he'll attack the Halleck Ranch?" Alan asked.

"He might tonight, but we'll be ready for him if he does. He might think a night raid could work, but he's takin' a chance. He's got some good gunmen but they are not soldiers. Not capable of planning a battle scenario, just raid and shoot, like an' Indian raid. He'll most likely try to hit us tomorrow, early. What I'm thinking of doing is, the men we deputize today, I'll have Greg and Ronnie bring them from the west side at day break tomorrow morning. We and the Halleck men, or gals, will hit from the east side and catch them in a pincer move like we did in the cavalry Alex."

"Sounds like a good plan Ed," Alex replied, "Just like Jeb Stewart would have planned."

"Exactly Alex, I think it will catch him off guard."

They finished their breakfast and Marshall Buist went to the sheriff's office to send a telegram to head quarters. He got Mr. Hays from the store to send it for him. Ed returned to the Black Steer and it was nearly nine o'clock.
"Mr. Volsch will you announce to the towns folk to meet with us?"
"Yes Sir Marshal, I told them I'd ring the bell."
With that Don went out and rand the bell on the saloon porch. There were several men in the saloon already but when Don rang the bell several more came to the Black Steer. Marshall Ed Buist was surprised how many came in through the batwing doors. All together he had twenty eight men standing there.
"Men, the day of Mark Hayes running this town, and this territory is over." Ed told them. "I am very happy to see you want to help and we need ya'."
"Not so fast," One man in the crowd said, "What's the chances we don't get the job done? With the killers he's got working for him, he'll wipe this town off the map, an' kill us all if we fail."
"I know your concern," Marshal Buist said, "But I have already notified the U.S. Marshall's office of our plan and they will send the Calvary before he can retaliate against you if I don't contact them by tomorrow night."
At that all the men in the saloon started taking among themselves. Then Don Volsch spoke up; "Yall' better get behind these men. For the first time in over a year someone has decided to help us. We in turn need to help them. You can count me in Mr. Buist."

"Me to, me to, and me." The men in the room started to say as they put up their hands to be recognized.
"OK then, step forward and raise your right hand," Marshal Buist told them, "I'm gonna' deputize yall' and you, all but five, will be under the command of Sheriffs Greg Bledsoe and Ronnie Hall. Five of you I want to come with me to the Halleck Ranch." Ed picked five men to join his group, then he got with Greg to finalize the time of the job at task. With that Marshal Buist, Alan, Alex, Bruce and the five men picked went out and mounted up for the ride to the Halleck Ranch.

Chapter Twenty Two

Haley Hunter asked Sabrina how her brother was doing.
"He's resting now, Haley, I got him stitched up. He lost a lot of blood and has a light fever, but I think he's gonna' be OK."
"Oh that's good news. I hope he pulls through OK. Thanks so much for all you did."
"He's gonna' be a little weak for a while and it's gonna' take him some time to recover fully. When he wakes I'll see if I can get some soup into him."
"Let me know when I can talk with him." Haley said and went out and joined the other gals in the yard.
Phil asked Haley how her brother was doing and she told him all she knew and thanked him for asking. Sam had the whole ranch on high alert, as he had not heard anything from Alan and the other with him. About ten o'clock two riders rode into the ranch yard, and Sam walked up to see what they wanted.
"What can I do for fella's?" Sam asked.
"Two of our riders came here yesterday and we ain't heard from them."
"Well one of them you ain't gonna' hear from an' the other is here but he's not going nowhere any time soon." Sam answered.
"What ya' meaning?"
"Lets just say one decided to meet his maker an' the other is badly wounded and his sister is taking care of him."
"We want our man. We can take care of him!"

“Well lets just say he’s got all the care he can get, so you boys can just mosey on out ta’ here.”
“Not without our man!” One of the riders said, and the two of them slid their hands to their guns. At that point there were enough clicks sounding like chickens pecking on an empty plate. Everyone in the yard had a gun cocked and pointing at the two men.
“We don’t have time to be takin’ care of anymore wounded,” Sam told them, “So ride on out or you can join the other man with your maker.”
The men looked and saw they were completely, even Samara on the porch had a rifle pointed at then.
“We’ll be back, my friend but you going to meet your maker real soon.” One of the men said and they turned their horses and trotted off. Sam just smiled and gave all in the yard a thumbs up sign.
Shortly after that Alan and the others came into the yard. They dismounted and Alan asked the crew to help get the five men takin care of, and then went to house to tell Samara of the plans for the morning raid. Samara asked Ed and the other lawmen to join her and Alan for lunch. Molly brought out a bottle of whisky and some ice for cocktails which all enjoyed. They were finishing lunch when Haley knocked on the open door frame.
“Come in Haley, is all OK?” Samara asked.
“Yes boss but my brother is awake and wants to talk to the Marshal. He said it was very, very important.”
“Well I better see what he wants.” Ed said. Any of ya’ wanta’ join me?” Of Course everyone wanted to go with him.

When they got to bunkhouse Sabrina said, "Whoa yall', the man wants' to talk to the Marshal. This ain't no family meetin'."
Alan, the marshal and Samara were allowed in to see Hunter. Ed walked up to him and asked, "You wanta' see me son?"
Hunter opened his eyes and looked up at Ed.
"Marshal……I,….I need to tell you something."
"Go ahead my boy, I'm right here."
"Mark…ah….pistol…. whipped…..Tom..ah…Wyler..inta' signin' that sale paper. Then…he, Mark…an' two men rode him to outside town…..an….shot him full of holes…to make it look….as a robbery. Mrs. Wyler an' her son young…Tom were visiting some friends an' dint know what tooked place."
"Well son, that's a big help. I thank you."
"There's ….there's more marshal…ah…Miss Samara's father, he….he was killed by Mark when…her dad caught Mark coming out ta' the canyon crack. I heard him tell….a…a....couple of the men."
Samara went white with a mixture of hate and relief. Finally the truth was brought out. She tanked Hunter and told him to let her know if he needed anything.
"Thank you…..ma'am…can I stay here with my sister?"
'Yes you can, Hunter as long as you want."
They left Hunter to rest. "Well we got what we need now ma'am," Marshal Buist said, "We can convict him on two counts of murder. As soon as we get this over we need to tell Mrs. Wyler and her son the ranch was still their ranch."

Things were falling in place very nicely now. All they had to do now is get Mark Hayes into custody.
Samara and Alan went back the main house to relax.
"Alan, I knew it all along. I knew in my heart that Mark killed my dad."
"We have proof and a witness now boss."
"I hope we can catch and bring him to trial, Alan. I want to watch him squirm with worry about hanging by the rope."
"it wont take long for a jury to settle on a verdict boss. But we gotta' catch him first."
"Unless I get a shot at him first Alan. I would love that even more."
"Boss lady, you ain't going on this raid. It's liable to be a hot fight an' I don't want you hurt."
Samara looked at Alan with a sort of smile. "Alan you worry about me a lot don't you?"
"Yes ma'am I do."
"Why Alan?"
"You're a special lady, you're beautiful, smart and you have a warm heart."
Samar walked to Alan and put her arms around him and looked him in the eyes. "How do you know I have a warm heart, Alan Holt?" She said in a soft voice. Her eyes seemed to be looking through him. "I'm falling for you Alan."
Alan held her and gave her a long heavy kiss. She was breathing heavily and was kissing back. Suddenly Samara broke free, ran to her bedroom and shut the door.

Alan thought, "What happened?" He walked to the door and asked what was wrong. "Leave me be, I'll see you at supper."

Alan shook his head and looked to the ceiling. As he was washing up for dinner he was thinking about Samara, she was a great kisser. "I could go for a lot more of that." He thought to himself, but what made her run away?

Samara sat on the edge of her bed thinking of what a fool she just made of herself. Good Lord, I'm falling in love, she thought. He's going to think I've lost my mind. I'm sure he likes me, but is it love or just lust. I know I'm not bad to look at, daddy always told me I was beautiful, but that was dad. I've had two men cheat on me and I can't face that again. Was it because I'm not as lovely as dad said? I try to be sincere.....

Ed Buist and the other lawmen can in for dinner and Samara greeted them and offered drinks. Samara had on a nice frilly blouse and a riding skirt. She really looked fresh and alive.

Alan came out of his room and he looked at how nice Samara was dressed. She turned and looked at Alan and thought, he was a good looking strong man, she enjoyed him being here. They all sat down for dinner and Samara sat next to Alan instead of across from him. Alan liked that.

Most every time she spoke to Alan she put her hand on his knee. Over dinner they talked about the plans for capturing Mark Hayes. Marshal Buist told them they would have to get up early because he wanted to be at the Hayes Ranch at daybreak. After dinner, they thanked Samara and Molly for the very good dinner and retired for the evening.

Samara and Alan helped Molly clean up the table and Molly told them she would wash the dishes with breakfast plates. Samara and Alan stood by her bedroom door and they looked at each other with searching eye's.
"Alan, I'm so sorry to have been so forward."
"I'm not boss, I've wanted to kiss you the first time I met you."
"You did not!"
"I did ma'am."
"Do you care for me Alan? I mean care, not just….."
"Yes ma'am, or boss, I do." Alan pulled her tight and kissed her warmly. Samara looked up with tears in her eyes. "Alan you can call me Samara, not boss, or ma'am."
He looked at her and replied, "Yes ma'am….ah..Samara."
She kissed him and said good night. Neither of them got to sleep quickly. They both had a lot on their minds and a lot of thinking to do.

Chapter Twenty Three

The morning seemed to come very early today. Molly had coffee ready and biscuits with gravy. Everyone ate hurriedly and Samara put on her jacket.
'You're not going ma'am." Alan told her.
"And why not?"
"I wont have you hurt, injured or possibly killed. I can't live with that."
"You do care, don't you Alan?"
"Yes Samara I do. Now sit tight here. Molly, hold her guns! I'm gonna tell Mr. Windy not to let you have a horse too!"
"Your getting awful bossy Alan. Remember I'm still the boss here until we're married!" With that her face went red and her mouth dropped open in surprise. Alan smiled, "That will my most wonderful day Miss Samara." She ran to him and kissed him heavily. Molly was smiling from ear to ear. "Please be careful Alan."
"I will my lovely lady." Alan tipped his hat and went out to mount up with others.
"Molly, I'm so afraid," Samara said, "I think I've met the man I've wanted and needed. I don't want to lose him."
"Don't you worry none Missy, he'll be just fine. I'll talk to the heavenly father to watch over him."
Samara went to her room and she prayed and she cried.

Alan, Ed and the others were loaded for bear as they rode west. It would take almost an hour to get to the Hayes Ranch and that would be daybreak, perfect timing. The air

was cool but when the sun rose it wouldn't take long for that to change. Alan's horse Buddy seemed to know something was up. His nostrils' were flared and his ears were pointed ahead as if seeking for signs. They rode on making good time. They got to within two hundred yards of the main house and pulled in their reins.
"Pretty quiet." Alan said to Ed.
"Ya', to quiet my friend. Hope Greg and Ronnie are in place." The Marshal answered.
"I'm sure they are Ed, I got a feeling they are looking forward to this."
"OK men let's move forward slowly and be alert." Ed told the men and they started moving. Suddenly some men were coming out of the barn and some from the house and gunfire erupted everywhere. Greg and his men charged forward firing in all directions. The Hayes men fought tough and several of their men were face down on the ground. As quick as it started it was over. The remaining Hayes men dropped their guns and held up their hands.
"Where's Mark Hayes?" Marshal Ed Buist hollered.
"Ain't seen 'em," One of the men answered, "He ain't here, left last night."
"Damn it," Ed said, "Where the hell did he go?"
"Don't rightly know. Rode off alone." The man replied.
"He couldn't have gone to town," Ed said to Alan, "He would have run into Greg and the boys. So where did he run off too?" They checked the house just to make sure. Mark was not there. Some of the deputized men were wounded, none seriously, and they didn't have anyone down. The marshal told the Hayes men to saddle up and get

out. “I want you men to start riding an’ don’t stop till you’re out of Texas. And don’t come back or I’ll personally shoot you myself.” The Hayes men saddled up and headed north in a hurry.

“Just where did he go?” The marshal murmured to himself.

Ed asked several of the towns men if they knew where Mrs. Wyler and her son were staying. A couple of them said they knew and Ed told them to tell her the Ranch was back in her hands and she could come home. Hopefully she could get some of her men to come back and work. Then Ed thanked all that was there for their help and the crowd gave a big cheer and waved their hats. Ed told Greg and Ronnie to hold the town until Ranger McHenry could get there to appoint a new sheriff.

“OK men, we now have a manhunt on our hands,” Ed told them, “We gotta’ find him and bring him in.”

They turned and started back to the Halleck Ranch. Ed had told Greg and Ronnie to be on the lookout just in case Mark tried to come to town and hire men for more trouble.

Alan was thinking of where Mark could have gone. Did he make a run for it? He wouldn’t have tried to go to Mexico. That was a long journey knowing that all Texas Rangers would be looking for him and he stood out unless he changed his appearance. But Mark Hayes didn’t until now ever show any fear. He thought he could handle anything.

Alan thought it over and over and an idea came to him.

“Ed I got to check something out. I’m going to the canyon crack and have a look around.”

“OK Alan, I’ll go with you.”

"No Ed, it won't take long for me to look things over. If I find anything I'll let you know."
"Don't take any chances Alan. He's dangerous, I don't like you gong with no backup."
"I won't Marshal, I just might have an idea. It's worth a check."
"Don't try to take him alone, Alan."
"OK Ed, I'll be careful."
Alan rode off heading north. Marshal Ed Buist and the rest rode for the Halleck Ranch. When they arrived Ed hollered,
"We need some help with the wounded."
Sabrina came out of the bunkhouse to see what she could do. She took a quick look at the wounded men and saw none were hurt seriously.
"Get me hot water," Sabrina ordered, "and plenty of fresh linen." Several of the gals and Sam helped the men to the bunkhouse. Samara looked into the yard and didn't see Alan. Her face went white with shock. "Oh good heavens." She screamed and ran out into the yard.
"Alan, Alan, where's Alan?"
"Hold on there miss," Ed said to her, "He's OK ma'am. He's just fine, not a scratch on him. He said he had to check on something."
"Where did he go?"
"He said he was going to the canyon ma'am."
"Did you get Mark?
"No ma'am, he wasn't there and we don't have any idea where he is."
"Oh no marshal, he can't take Mark, Mark will kill him!"

"He just said he was gonna' have a look around Miss Halleck. He isn't going to do anything foolish."
"Phil, saddle up my horse please." Samara ordered.
"Where you going, ma'am?" Ed asked.
"I'm going to find him, Mark will kill him, I know it."
"Well I can't stop ya', but I'll get Sam Griffin and we'll ride with you."
"OK marshal, I'll get my rifle." Samara got her rifle and the three of them mounted up and started for the canyon.

Chapter Twenty Four

As Alan was riding to the canyon he noticed fresh tracks heading the same way. I figured so, Alan thought, and let Buddy have his head. He got about a quarter mile from the canyon crack and the tracks were still going in the same direction. The tracks were from a big horse, one like Mark Hayes rode. Alan looked around and when he turned back there was an old Indian man standing in front of him, holding a walking stick. Alan's horse Buddy hated Indian but Buddy paid him mind, like he wasn't even there.

Where did he come from? Alan thought? I should have seen him before this.

"Greetings my son," the old Indian said, "Are you going to the sacred passage?"

"I'm heading for the crack in the canyon wall."

"You must know my son that inside that canyon is where slain warriors go to rest. It is sacred ground. If you go there in peace they will pay you no mind. You must remember not to deface the prayer poles. Your future wife's father never did. He honored the spirits of the dead.

"Did you know Mr. Halleck? And how do you know his daughter will be my wife?"

"I know him well, a honest man he is, there is much I know Alan. You must know there are treasures in there, but don't be greedy as the warriors spirits will take revenge. You may take a little at a time, Cliff Halleck did so."

"I thank you for the information old man, but where did you come from?" The old Indian raised his staff to the sky.

"I must warn you my son. There is danger in that passage waiting for you. Be careful and believe in the Great Spirit in the sky to protect you."

Alan looked at the crack in the canyon and when he looked back the old Indian was gone. It put a chill up his spine. He spurred Buddy to move forward, but Buddy just snorted, he did not want to go. "Come on Buddy, let's get a moving."

Buddy moved forward but not in his usual gate. Buddy sensed something, Alan could tell. But why, as much as he hated Indians, did he not react to the old man? He was an Indian.

Buddy moved forward but it was like he was walking on eggs. When they got to the crack Buddy stopped. His nostrils were flared and his ears were pointed straight ahead. He sensed danger and did not want to go in there.

After much prodding and pleading Buddy started into the crack, but he didn't like it one bit. The crack was just wide enough for a man on a horse to pass through. Alan's boots would scrape the walls in places. And there was not enough room to turn your horse around if you had to. There was no backing out unless it got wider. Alan noticed a lot of quartz in the rock walls and here and there a slash of bright yellow. The canyon crack was very cool and not much daylight came into it. Alan rode for what seemed like forever, although it was but maybe ten minutes and it suddenly opened up. The opening was roughly three hundred feet deep and seventy five feet wide. There were prayer sticks with feathers, furs and ribbons all over the ground. There was buffalo, antelope and human bones all over the ground. He also noticed chunks of topaz lying everywhere. Then Alan saw a big sorrel horse tied to a juniper, but no man in sight. Suddenly there was the crack of a pistol and Alan felt like he was hit in the shoulder by a pool ball. Buddy reared up, and Alan jumped off Buddy. Alan was hit in the shoulder but luckily it didn't hit any bone. It was bleeding, but not real serious, bad enough though. Buddy nudged him as if to say, lets get out of here. Alan couldn't get to his rifle so he pulled his pistol. He still couldn't see where the shot came from, but he knew the man would have to get to his horse or kill Alan first. Buddy grabbed Alan by his shirt and tried to get him up.

"Get back Buddy," he said, "Get out the way, I don't want you getting hurt Buddy." Alan crawled behind a large rock for protection.

"Throw out your gun and stand up." The man shooting at him hollered.

"Not on you life Hayes." Alan answered.

"You ain't gonna' go no where cowpoke. I know you. You're the drifter that asked for a job. Should a' taken that job, you'd been better off."

"Don't think so fella," Alan replied, "Your men gave up an' quit, you ain't got a ranch anymore."

Alan heard Mark Hayes curse profusely. Suddenly Buddy sensed something and backed up. Mark Hayes ran for his horse but before Alan could shoot there was the crack of a rifle and Mark went down.

Alan rolled over and there was Samara standing there with her Henry Rifle in her hands. She saw Alan and ran over to him.

"Oh Alan, you've been shot. Let me look at it." She pulled Alan's shirt back and gasped. "Good heavens Alan, my love, you're hurt."
"Not to serious dear, I'll make it."
Samara kissed and held him in her arms. Marshal Buist and Sam came up to them. "Looks like you got him young lady. Nice shooting." Sam walked over to Mark and turned him over.
"He's still alive!" Sam shouted. Samara grabbed her rifle and said; "Let me finish him off."
"Hold on there missy," Ed said, "Let the law take care of this now. He'll hang, I swear he will."
"Let me kill the low life slimy bastard." Samara answered.
"No ma'am, I'll take it from here. Sam get him on his horse." Sam tried but he couldn't get Mark on his horse, Mark was just to big for him to handle alone, so Ed helped him.
"I knew you were coming here Alan, and I just knew it was going to go wrong."
"Glad you did Samara. He had me cornered but when he saw you, Sam and Ed he went for his horse. I don't know where he thought he was going to go."
"We met an old Indian man before we entered the canyon crack and he told me my husband was in here, and the Great Spirit was watching over you."
"Your husband?'
"Any complaints about that Alan?'
"No ma'am… ah...Samara, that will be the happiest day of my life. I fell in love with you the first I saw you."

"Just remember, I'm still the boss till we get married Alan."

"You'll always be the Boss sweetheart, that will never change."

They all started for the ranch with Mark handcuffed to his horse, bleeding badly. When they arrived at the ranch everyone came to meet them and congratulated them on the capture of Mark Hayes.

"Let Sabrina have a look at him." Ed asked

Sabrina came and looked at Mark. "That's a serious wound marshal. That bullet has to come out if we're gonna' save him."

"Do what you gotta' do lady," Ed told her, "Just make sure it hurts like hell." Marshal Ed went into the bunkhouse as they carried Mark in and handcuffed him to the bunk they put him in.

"This place is turning into a damn hospital." Sabrina said as she went into the bunkhouse.

Samara helped Alan to the house and Molly saw he was wounded. "I'll get some hot water and some bandages Missy. Don't you worry we'll get him fixed up."

Ed wrote a note and asked Windy if he would go to Hays Town and send a telegraph to the U.S. Marshall's head-quarters in Wichita, Kansas, telling them he got Mark Hayes.

Samara and Molly cleaned Alan's wound and wrapped it up. "He's gonna be OK missy," Molly said, "Guess I'll start getting what I need to makin' a cake."

"A cake, what for."

"For the wedding Missy, you're big day."

Samara smiled and hugged Alan. "I finally found my man Alan. I'll make you happy."
"I'm gonna' do all I can to make you happy to sweetheart, I promise."
"You will Alan, I know you will."
Alan spent the rest of the day resting with Samara looking over him like an old mother hen. Molly was so happy that Samara had finally found a good man she could trust. Molly thought it was about time.
Around five o'clock Molly asked Samara when did she want to have dinner and how many to prepare for.
"Make something simple for tonight Molly, there will be six for dinner. Tomorrow afternoon we will have a cookout for every one. I'll have Phil and Windy make it up with some help from the gals. That will give you a break and you're invited too, of course!"
"Thank you Missy, it sounds like fun. By the way Miss Samara, have you and Mr. Allen set a date for the big day yet? I'll need time to make you a lovely cake."
Alan heard the conversation from his place on the couch and hollered; "Tomorrow will be fine with me Molly!"
Samara and Molly laughed,
"You'll need a couple of days of rest and recuperation Alan," Samara said as she walked to him, "That was a bad hit you took. Besides, you're gonna' need all the strength you can muster for your wedding night!" Molly let out a big laugh.
"I think it'll be in a couple of weeks Molly." Samara said.
"A week, at most Molly! Alan replied. Samara shook her head, smiled and kissed Alan and said; "OK Alan."

Summary

Well it looks as though things are working out real good for this part of Texas. Hays Town is going to get an honest sheriff and business can go on without fear of Mark Hayes telling them what they could or could not do. The Wyler's got their ranch back and a lot of the good cowmen that once worked for them came back on to work the herd and keep the ranch up. The Marshalls Ed Buist, Alex Schuring and Texas Ranger Bruce McHenry got their man and as soon as Hayes was able to travel he was going to the nearest courthouse to stand trial.

Alan and Samara were going to be married and what a nice couple they will make. Samara finally got a man she could depend on and one she could trust as well. Alan was getting the woman of his dreams.

It looks as though there will be good times to be had by all from now on. After all what could possibly go wrong?

Chapter Twenty Five

The next day was busy. Phil and Windy with help from the gals were preparing for the big shindig celebration. Alan was still in bed when Samara brought him coffee and breakfast. Alan tried to complain but it did him no good. Marshal Ed Buist went in to check on Mark Hayes and Sabrina told him he was doing OK so far, that it would take some time. He told her to keep him informed and don't take any chances with him.

Sam took Marks saddle bags to the house to show Alan and Samara their contents. They were full of gold nuggets the size of marbles and a large quantity of Topaz of all sizes. A small fortune was in those saddle bags.

Alan remarked what the old Indian said about being greedy. The spirits of the warriors would have revenge. And so they did.

"We need to take those to an assay office and change that into cash." Samara said.

"I think to be on the safe side of those avenging warriors' spirits we need to save half for ourselves and split the other half with the hired hands." Alan replied.

"That's a good idea, Alan." Samara answered, "They earned it for sure."

"Wow," Sam said, "Thanks, that's great of you Alan, Samara, that'll be more money then I've ever had. And the others will really appreciate it too, I'm sure."

"You're welcome Sam. You worked for it." Samara told him.

That gave Alan something to do. He sat in a chair and started dividing the treasure as evenly as he could.

The weather was overcast, so it was cooler outside than it would have been if the sun was beating down. At about five, Phil rang the bell to let all know the meal was ready to serve. He had roasted a hog over the hot coals and a large pot of barbeque beans an onions.

Samara had gotten Windy to go to the Black Steer, in Hays Town and bring back two barrels of beer which he had covered in hay to keep it cool. He also took a copper coil from a moonshine still he had and put it a bucket packed with ice so the beer would cool even more when it was drawn.

Samara said grace and Phil started carving.

"Shame Greg an' Ronnie are gonna' miss this," Sam said.

"They should be here any minute," Windy replied, "I told 'em Miss Samara and Alan wanted them to be here. Don, the owner of the Black Steer said he and his shotgun would act as sheriff till they got back." Marshal Ed got a laugh from that remark.

The beer was cold and the pork and beans were done to perfection. Windy started to play his accordion and the toes were just a tapping. Some of the gals grabbed Greg, Ronnie, Alex, Bruce, Ed and were dancing around the fire pit. The other gals were butting in from time to time. All were having a good time. Molly had drank a couple of beers and was feeling pretty good. She grabbed Marshal Ed and started dancing with him. Ed being the gentleman he was went along with it nicely. All got a chuckle over that.

"Today is Tuesday," Samara said to Alan, "How about Sunday?"
"Sunday for what dear?"
"Alan, you changed your mind about our wedding?"
"Oh, I'm sorry Hun, I wasn't thinking."
"Guess not. A couple of hours ago I thought I was going to have to beat you outta' tomorrow." They kissed warmly.
The party went on for hours. There had been plenty to eat and the beer was refreshing. All were having fun. It was such a relief that all the hate and fear was over. Marshal Ed was just waiting for Mark to recover enough to travel, and then he could start on a new case. There was enough lawlessness in Texas, Oklahoma, and Kansas to keep him, Alex and other U.S. marshals busy for quite awhile. Texas Ranger McHenry and all the other rangers had plenty to do in Texas. One by one they all were starting to retire for the evening. Samara had already got Alan to go to bed as she could see he was tiring. Molly was passed out on her bed with her dress still on, Samara laughed and closed her door, then she to retired.
It was about three in the morning Samara was wakened by a commotion outside. She put on her robe and went to the door to examine what was cause. Sam came to the porch.
"Ma'am, Mark Hayes has escaped."
"What! You're joking of course."
"I wouldn't joke about that ma'am."
"Oh Good Lord, does Marshal Ed know?"
"They are waking him now ma'am."
"How did he get away? He was handcuffed to the bed?"
"I don't know ma'am, were trying to find Sabrina."

"Sabrina is missing too?"
"Yes ma'am and Phil is missing also."
"Let me get dressed, I'll be out in a minute."
Samara quickly got dressed and ran out to the bunkhouse.
"What the hell!" Samara could here Ed say. "How'd he get loose?"
They looked around and searched the bunks, the yard and the barn. Mark's horse and saddle were also missing.
Margaret hollered from the bunk outhouse, "Over here, it's Phil."
Everyone ran to check on Phil, he was knocked out cold. The hand cuffs were on the floor next to him.
Sabrina was nowhere to be found.
After some cold towels on his head Phil regained conciseness.
"What the hell happened?" Marshal Ed asked.
"Sabrina woke me, and said that Mark had to use the toilet. So I got my pistol, unlocked him from the bed and cuffed his wrists together and put the keys in my vest pocket. I escorted him to relieve himself. He went inside and still had his cuffs on so I stepped outside. I heard a noise that sounded like he fell so I opened the door. I didn't see him and before I could turn I felt a blow and saw a white flash."
"Damn it!" Ed said.
"I'm sorry Marshal, I didn't think he was healthy enough to cause trouble."
"It's OK Phil, you didn't know, can't blame you." Ed replied. "We gotta' find him and Sabrina too!"
Samara was sickened. "I should a' killed him when I had the chance." She said.

“We’ll find him ma’am,” Ed told her, “We’ll get ‘em.”
Ole man Windy was a pretty good tracker so he saddled his horse and Marshal Ed, Sam, and Ranger McHenry joined him and they started looking for Marks trail. The big sorrel Mark rode left an easy track to follow. It headed due west. They first thought he was going to what was his ranch, but the trail dropped down south west. They came to a wide stream and when they got to the other side they couldn’t pick up Marks trail.
“Musta’ went up or down stream to hide his trail,” Windy said, “Lets split up inta’ pairs. Each man ride on the opposite side of the stream till we find where he got out.”
Marshal Ed and Sam went north, and Windy and Ranger Bruce, went south. “Whistle when you find his mark.” Windy told them, and they started looking. They rode on both sides of the stream for miles with no track to be found of Marks horse. Finally Windy gave up. “He couldn’t have rode this stream forever.” Windy said. “He had to of pulled a fast one. But what I don’t rightly know. I’m gonna back track.”
Windy and the ranger slowly went back looking for any blade of bent grass. Texas Ranger Bruce McHenry was a good tracker himself. He had to be, to find wanted men in the vast badlands of Texas. He too was baffled. Marshal Buist was wondering the same thing.
“He had to cross somewhere Sam, but where?”
“Your right Mr. Ed, but the only thing I saw was where a herd of cattle crossed and there were no horse tracks with them.”

Windy and Bruce caught up with Ed and Sam and they decided to make some coffee and talk it over.

"Ain't like he done jus' disappeared," Windy told them as they were drinking coffee, "He's pulled a fast one on us an' we gotta' figure out what."

"I'd hate to think he's gonna' pull it off, Windy." Ed said.

"If we don't come up with something soon," Bruce answered, "He just might."

"Damn it!" Marshal Ed Buist exclaimed, "Damn it to hell boys."

Sam looked east and saw a rider coming. It wasn't Mark Hayes though, it was Marshal Alex Schuring. Alex pulled up and asked, "How's it going men?"

"Not so good fella', seems we lost his trail." Windy told him. "We gotta' keep lookin'."

Alex pulled out his cup and poured a cup of coffee and sat down on his heels. Sam told Windy, "The only thing I saw was where a cattle herd crossed. That's all I saw."

"Cattle crossed?" Windy asked Sam.

"Yes sir bout a half a mile back."

"That just might be it." Windy replied. "Ole Indian trick. They would get inta' a herd of buffalo and ride with 'em to hide their horse's tracks. We gotta' check it out."

They finished their coffee, put the fire out and mounted up to have a closer look at the cattle crossing.

Chapter Twenty Six

Samara told Alan what happened and he was fit to be tied. He wanted to saddle up Buddy and take after Windy and the group but Samara would have no part of it and ordered him back the house. "You can't go out there wounded as you are Alan."

"Honey I just can't sit here with Mark on the loose. Ain't no tellin' what he will do."

"Well your gonna' have to sit here Alan, cause I'm still the boss remember?"

Alan sat in a chair and looked out the window. Samara felt for him as she knew he felt like he should be out there looking, but she didn't want his wound to open or get infected. And more over, she didn't want Mark Hayes killing him. Alan's a strong man and may be quick with his gun, she thought, but she had a fear in her heart and didn't want to take any chances. She knew his manly pride was hurt. But he was still alive, and if she hadn't shot Mark when she did, he might have killed Alan. Samara walked over to Alan, kissed him and rubbed his head. He looked at Samara and smiled. She knew how he felt. She was proud of him.

Phil was feeling bad about Mark escaping and was taking it hard. And the fact that Sabrina was missing only added to his misery. The wounded men from town got on their horses and started to ride back to town. They traveled several miles and they saw a flock of buzzards hovering in the distance. Being curious they decided to check it out. They couldn't believe what they found. It was Sabrina hanging from a tree. When they got there they found she was still alive. Barely! She was hanging from her wrist tangled in the rope above her head. They untied the rope and gave her some water. She drank so fast she choked on the water, coughing and trying to catch her breath.

They asked Sabrina what had happened. She told them that Mark had tied her hands, then put the rope over her neck and pulled just tight enough that it left some slack in it and tied it off. Sabrina told them Mark said he didn't want to kill her outright because she had doctored him up. Sabrina told them Mark had told her he would let nature take its course.

Sabrina then told them she was getting tired so she managed to get her hands untied but she didn't have enough rope to get where Mark had tied it off. Mark also had tied the rope around her neck in a knot she couldn't get undone. But she could reach up and loop her wrist in it as she knew sooner or later she would pass out and she finally did. Having her wrist looped in the rope kept her from being strangled.

The men couldn't believe how ruthless Mark Hayes was to leave a woman out here to choke to death. One of the men put Sabrina on his horse with him and told the others he would take her back to the Halleck Ranch. She was a lucky lady!

Windy finally found Marks trail and as they were following it looked as it was leading them to Hays Town. Ed couldn't believe it. By the time they got to town it was getting late.

They rode up to the sheriff's office and found Ronnie in the office playing solitaire.

"Howdy," Ronnie said as they walked in, "What brings you fellas' to our quiet little town?"

"Might not be quiet for long Ronnie," Ed answered, "Mark escaped, and it looks like he's around here somewhere."

"You're kidding Marshal. Here in town?"

"Damned if I'd be kidding about such a thing son."

"Well marshal he didn't just come a walkin' inta' town. Greg an' I would have seen him for sure."

"He's around here or near by Ronnie. We better tell Greg quickly, and scour the town for clues."

They got with Greg and they started looking and asking questions. Windy went to the livery stable and found Mark's horse there. He asked the man in the stable how it got there.

"Some boy brought in here and said a big man with white hair paid him a dollar to bring it here."

"Do you know whose horse that is?" Windy asked him.

"Yeah, that's Mark Hayes horse he kept it hear all the time. And when the boy gave his description, I knew for sure."

"Why didn't you tell one of the two sheriffs?"

"I was getting to fella', but I wasn't about to go running down the street an' get shot. I gotta' a family to tend for. An that man's a killer."

All the lawmen were going from door to door searching for Mark but he was not found. They told the folks to be very alert. Marshal Ed figured Mark was holed up somewhere outside of town waiting for an opportune moment.

"OK," Ed said, "I want someone on the street at all times. Work in shifts. When it gets dark a couple of us will go out and check the wooded areas around town. He might make a fire and we can spot that."

"I don't think he'll be dumb enough to make a fire," Alex replied, "He's to smart for that."

"You right, Alex, I guess he's smarter than that, but we'll check anyway."

"I want one man on each end of town tonight," Ed told them, 'Sooner or later he'll make a mistake."

"We better alert the folks when they come into town." Ranger Bruce said. And with that they started preparing for a long night. They grabbed a quick bite at the Black Steer and told Don to be on the lookout. Don smiled and showed his double barrel shotgun. "We'll be a ready," He told them, "Jess don't wanta' mess up my floor again, but I guess it'll be worth it." Ranger McHenry and Sam Griffin took the first shift, and Marshals Buist and Schuring walked out to the woodland outside of town to poke around for clues.

Everyone was overjoyed to see Sabina was OK. She had been ruffed up a little, but not injured. Sabrina ate a little bit, took a drink of wine and went to rest for the evening.

Alan was a mess. He was hoping to hear some news by now. His nerves were a wreck. Alan and Samara had a drink together and ate their meal. Alan wasn't very talkative. Samara tried to comfort Alan as she knew how he felt. They kissed warmly and went off to bed.

Chapter Twenty Seven

Samara woke up early and went to check on Alan and change his bandages. She went into his room and Alan was not in bed. She went to the kitchen to see if he was having coffee. Not there either. So she walked out to the bunkhouse, and as she looked at the corral, Buddy was gone!

"Damn it," she muttered, "Should a' hog tied him in bed."

"Phil, saddle my horse please." Samara asked.

She mounted up and started looking for Buddy's tracks. It didn't take long to find Alan's trail. It looked as though he was heading to the canyon. Samara spurred her horse and rode after him. She was mad, concerned, worried, and ready to have a hissy fit.

Alan rode to the canyon and was looking for tracks from Mark's horse, but he wasn't finding any. He turned and the old Indian was standing there. Buddy never moved or paid the old man any mind at all.

"You look in vain my son, he is not there." He said to Alan. "You will not find him my son he will find you!"

"How do you know that?" Alan asked.

"I know much my son. You will have a long wonderful life, a loving wife, and children to carry on your lines, but be alert on your wedding day!"

"Thank you sir, I will." Suddenly the old Indian disappeared, Buddy never moved but Alan couldn't believe his eyes. He just vanished.

Alan looked over his shoulder and saw a rider coming hard and fast. He pulled his rifle at the ready and cocked it.

As the rider closed in Alan saw it was Samara. Boy your in trouble, he thought.
Samara rode to him and pulled up her horse. He could tell she was angry.
"Alan, just what in the hell do you think your doing? Sneaking out of the house, not telling me where your going and with old wrapping on your wound. I'm madder than a wet hen."
"Honey, if I told you what I was doing you wouldn't me out of the house."
"Exactly Alan, why did you come here alone? Looking for Mark?"
"Yes, I thought he might have come here to hide."
"And what were going to do? Shoot it out with him? Wounded and all. I want you in one piece for our wedding this Sunday. Know Buddy will you get my man home so I came spank him." Buddy looked at Samara, turned and started back for the ranch. It was a quiet ride. Alan tried to talk but Samara told him to shut up and ride.

Mr. Hays walked into the sheriff's office. All the lawmen were there talking. None of them saw anything suspicious all night.
"Marshal," Mr. Hays said, "Someone broke into my store last night and took two pistols, a double holster belt and a box of fifty bullets."
"Damn it," Marshal Buist swore, "How'd' he do that right under our noses?"
"We had someone on the street all night Marshal." Greg replied.

"OK, let's go have a look around boys." They all went to Hays's store to see what they could learn. Whoever broke into the store came in through the back door. Windy Lee went around back to look for signs. He returned and reported his findings to Marshal Buist.

"Big heavy man it was," Windy told Ed, "deep foot prints in the sand. Good sized boot too!"

"How did sneak in an' out?" Ed asked.

"You got me," Marshal Alex said, "I didn't hear anything on my shift." The others agreed with Alex, they heard nothing either.

Ed Buist was bewildered as were the others. How did a man that big and heavy sneak into Mr. Hays store, forcing the back door, rummaging around in the dark and no one hearing anything? They all could not imagine how he did it! But, he sure did!

While they were going over the possibilities, the man from the livery stable walked in Hays store.

"Marshal, Mark Hayes's horse is gone."

"What ya' mean, gone?"

"Well I mean gone, not in the stable, like gone sir."

"This is getting to look like a three ring circus," Ed replied, "A two hundred fifty pound man sneaks into Mr. Hays store and rides out ta' town an' no one see's or hears nothing!" Marshal Buist was beside himself in anger.

"Well boss, I don't know how he did it," Marshal Schuring answered, "But if ya' don't see or hear nothing, how the hell are we suppose apprehend him?"

"We all took our watch," Ranger McHenry said, "An all seemed OK. An' I didn't doze off either."

"I didn't either." Greg replied. And Sam and Ronnie said the same. As Ed walked out of the store shaking his head he saw the young boy that brought Mark's horse to the stable walking by.

"How you doing son?"

"Just great sir, that big man with the white hair paid me two dollars to bring his horse to the fork in the road this morning."

"He did. When son?"

"I had to get up early sir, he wanted his horse at six this morning. He sure is a nice man. I made three dollars in two days." Ed shook his head and asked Windy to have the boy show him where he met Mark and see if he could find his trail. Marshal Ed then told Windy to come back to the sheriffs office an let him know what he found.

"Come on men, I don't know about you, but I need a drink." They all followed Ed to the Black Steer.

Chapter Twenty Eight

Samara and Alan rode into the ranch yard and dismounted. They unsaddled their horses and put them in the corral.

"Honey I'm sorry, I just couldn't sit by and not try to do my part."

"I know Alan, but do you realize who you were going after all alone?"

"I wasn't gonna' try to take him dear. I was just trying to locate him."

"And what if he saw you first, Alan? He would have killed you! Did you stop to think about that? I'm gonna' marry a man I fell in love with, with no warning, and I fell in love truly. I don't want that taken away."

"I'm sorry darling, I didn't mean to frighten or upset you."

"No you didn't stop to think about it Alan. You gotta' think of us as a team from now on. Now get washed up an' let me change those wrappings an' clean that wound."

Alan gave Samara a hug and went into the house. He washed up and Samara was waiting with Molly, fresh linen in hand. As they were dressing Alan's wound they remarked at how well it was healing. Alan told Samara about the old Indian and what he had said to him.

"That's mighty spooky Missy." Molly said.

"Yes indeed Molly. Wonder what he meant by being alert on our wedding day? Mark couldn't be that stupid to try something with all these lawmen, cowhands and half the town here."

"Well it must be gonna' turn out alright," Alan said, "The old man said we were going to have children."

"Yes we are Alan, yes we are. A boy for you and a darling little girl for me."
"Oh I can't wait for that Missy." Molly told Samara.
"Pretty sure of yourself, aren't you?" Alan said with a grin.
"Oh yes, my daddy said I was spoiled and always got what I wanted. I got you didn't I?" Samara smiled, kissed Alan and asked Molly to put a lunch together.

Windy found Marks trail but lost it. He told Marshal Buist that Mark had covered it somehow. Ed was disgusted, but determined to get Mark, somehow, but right now he wasn't sure just how.
The next couple of days passed by quietly. They searched the vast open areas but found no sign of Mark. He had just disappeared it seemed. The wedding was to take place on Sunday at two o'clock. That would give the pastor time to have his sermon at church and then come to the ranch. The whole town was invited and Don and Terri decided to close the Black Steer until Monday.
Phil and Windy with help from the girls were going to start a steer over the coals Saturday night. Everyone was excited and were getting their best duds to wear. The gals were repairing and exchanging dresses for the big day. Molly was getting the makings of the wedding cake ready so it would be done by the big day. Samara had picked out a lovely blue dress that she had saved from her mother's wardrobe. She kept thinking how nice it would have been if her Mom and Dad could be there. But then again she thought, yes, they will be there, she could feel it.

Saturday morning came and things around the ranch were very busy getting everything together and ready for the big day. All the lawmen were there as the word got out about what the old Indian had told Alan, and they were going to be ready. Marshal Ed had gotten with a couple of the gals and wanted them to be stationed with rifles. One on the water tower, and two in the barn, so they could cover the ranch yard, and the approach to it. The lawmen with, Sam, Greg and Ronnie were to be on the ground among the crowd. But everyone was thinking as Samara had thought. Why would Mark be that dumb, unless he had a death wish because he couldn't run this time?

It was a little after noon and Lisa Moody and Nicole Martin came riding into the yard.

"There's about twelve or so men and a wagon coming up the road to the ranch." Lisa told Sam.

Sam ordered everyone on hand to be ready as he had no idea who the riders were or what they wanted. He was sure it couldn't be Mark Hayes, but got ready just the same.

In about ten minutes several riders and a wagon pulled by four mules were coming through the gate. Sam had told Samara and she was standing in the doorway with Alan. They both had rifles at the ready. Not very often did a band of strangers stop by and it was best to be prepared.

One of the riders, a husky man, rode to the center of the yard and stopped. Samara looked at him and said, "Oh my heavens, it's Charlie Lassiter, what's he doing here?"

Samara ran out into the yard to meet him, Alan followed.

"What are doing here Mr. Lassiter? Haven't seen you in over a year."

"Sold some breeding cattle to John Witt, up in Wyoming Territory, on my way back home to my Becky. Thought I'd stop an' see Cliff an' you and have a drink with your ole man."

"Mr. Lassiter, Dad's dead, was murdered by a man named Mark Hayes about nine months ago."

"I'll be damned, ma'am, did they hang him?"

"The lawmen caught him but he got away. Their looking for him again."

"Well I'm sure glad I'm here, I'll damn sure help 'em look."

"I'm glad you're here to Mr. Lassiter. You're just in time for my wedding tomorrow. I want you to meet my soon to be husband, Alan Holt. Alan this is Mr. Charlie Lassiter, from Lufkin, Texas." Alan reached out his hand to shake with Charlie.

"Just call me Charlie, everyone one else does." Alan nodded at Lassiter.

"Well you and your men are invited to make your self at home Mr. Charlie. Were gonna' have plenty for all tomorrow." Samara told him. "Set up your camp behind the barn and y'all can use the wash house."

"Young lady let me know what I can do to help. My chuck wagon man there, is John Bolger, we call him cookie for short. He can help your folks prepare the fixins' an after the wedding me and my men will join the hunt for Cliff's killer."

As the men came riding in, Charlie introduced Alan and Samara to them.

“This here is my two sons, Brad and Steve,” the boys waved and tipped their hats.
“They are fifteen an’ fourteen, and this is their third drive.”
“You start ‘em early Mr. Charlie.”
“They gotta’ learn the business Missy, It’ll be theirs one day. This here is Cookie, John Bolger. Best chuck wagon man on the trail.”
“Howdy ma’am,” Cookie John said, “It’s easy when you got a good outfit to work with. It’s nice to meet you ma’am. And nice ta’ meet you Alan.”
Samara told Charlie to come to the house for a drink after he freshened up, and then went on to the house. She told Alan about Charlie, and his wife Becky, of being good friends of the family for years. Samara told Alan she could see that the news of her Dad’s death gripped Mr. Lassiter.
Charlie Lassiter came to the house and met with Samara and Alan. They sat down and Molly brought out some of Cliff’s bourbon.
Charlie took a sip and said, “Yer’ ole man could come up with the best whisky in the country. Ya’ need to try some of Cookie John’s brew, now that’s some good drink too!”
They started talking about old times when Charlie raised his hand and said; “I damn near forgot. Have ya’ heard the latest? General George Custer and his Seventh Calvary got wiped out by the Sioux, Cheyenne and Arapaho a week ago. I mean massacred ‘em!”
“Never would have thought that would of have happened to him.” Alan replied.
“Me neither son,” Charlie said, “We passed through the battle field a day after. There were mutilated dead all over

the place. I mean they were chopped up, dismembered, I mean ta' tell ya'."

"That's horrible Mr. Charlie," Samara said, "Did you run into any Indians?"

"We saw lots of 'em ma'am, but they were heading north. Didn't pay us any mind a tall."

"Must have been a sight," Alan said, "I've seen what they can do to a man. It's awful."

"It is at that young man. We found a Sioux warrior badly wounded, brought him with us. He's coming around pretty good."

"He didn't try to fight back or escape?" Samara asked.

"No Missy, Cookie speaks Sioux, and A K, as we call him, told Cookie John he wasn't for the battle in the first place, he was against it. If we didn't find him when we did he most certainly would have died. He's grateful to us and told me if he heals well, he'll work for me to repay his debt."

"Why do you call him A K?" Samara asked.

"His real name is, Akecheta Otaktay, and in Sioux it means, warrior that kills men. Says he got that name from battles with the Kiowa and the Cherokees. Most of the men can't pronounce his name so they just call him A K. You'll get to meet him."

"You actually trust him, and will have him work for you Mr. Charlie? I'd be fearful." Samara asked.

"Cookie John says he telling the truth. I'll give 'em a chance."

Cookie John gave Molly a smoked ham from an antelope he shot. Molly fixed it up with onions, carrots and cabbage. It turned out very tasty. Charlie, his two sons, Brad and

Steve, along with Marshal Ed Buist joined Samara and Alan for dinner. They talked old times and western adventures. Cattle drives, railroads, indians and the building of towns.
Finally Samara got up and thank all for having dinner and told Alan, "See ya' at two tomorrow honey!"
"Two! What do you mean two?"
"It's unlucky to see the bride before wedding time Alan." She gave him a kiss and wished all a good night and retired for the evening.

Charlie, Ed, and Alan sat and continued talking about old times, law and order nowadays and the Indian problems. The two boys, Brad and Steve went on the Lassiter camp. Charlie Lassiter told Marshal Ed Buist he and his men would stay and help in the search for Mark Hayes. Ed told Charlie he appreciated his willingness to help.
Finally after swapping tales they all decided to hit the sack and get some rest. Sunday was going to be a big day!

Chapter Twenty Nine

Alan woke up at dawn, got out of bed and stretched. He looked out the window and things were busy in the yard. The hands were getting ready to eat breakfast. Cookie John had brought his wagon next to the bunkhouse and was helping Phil and Windy make breakfast for the Halleck and Lassiter crews. The yard was full of people. The Lassiter crew was there, Greg, Ronnie and Sam making sure the yard was straight and clean. The wedding was to take place on the front porch of the main house and the gals had started decorating it with Ivy, Flowers and Ribbons.

Alan thought of what a wonderful day this would be. He was marrying the woman of his dreams. He also thought how lucky he had been to meet her as he did. And now to be part owner of a very successful cattle ranch, his roaming days were over. He just couldn't believe his luck. He thought of developing the herd even bigger and adding new breeds of cattle.

He got washed up and dressed, then went out to see what could be had for breakfast. Molly was coming out of Samara's room. "Mornin' Mr. Alan," Molly said, "I just took your honey her breakfast. Would you like yours now?"

"Yes I would Molly. What do you suggest?"

"Well, I made Missy flapjacks with honey an' butter an' bacon. Would you like the same?" Molly asked as she poured Alan a cup of coffee. "Do you want eggs too?"

"Pancakes and bacon sounds just fine Molly, thank you."

Alan sat and ate a large stack of pancakes and enjoyed his coffee. Molly asked to look at his wound. "That is healing real nicely Mr. Alan, how's it feeling?"
"A little sore, Molly, but other than that it feels a lot better, thanks to you and Samara." Molly smiled and excused herself.
"Gotta get busy for today, Mr. Alan. Got a lot to get ready."
Alan went outside and walked around talking to all that were there. In a couple of hours the folks from town will be coming in for the big shindig. Sam, Ronnie and Greg patted him on the back and told him how lucky he was. Of course Alan agreed with them. Marshal Buist and Charlie Lassiter congratulated Alan also. Looks like this was going to be a day to remember, Alan thought to himself. Cookie John Boger asked Alan if he wanted anything to eat.
"No thanks, but thanks for the offer, Molly cooked me a big breakfast, I'm stuffed."
Alan noticed Cookie had A K sitting on a blanket next to his wagon. Alan walked over to A K and gave him the peace greeting in Indian sign language. A K smiled and said good day in his Sioux language. Alan acknowledged with sign.

Things were very busy indeed. Some of the crew went into the house and brought the piano out onto the porch to play for the wedding. There were several musical instruments sitting there ready to play at a minutes notice. About one o'clock the towns people were beginning to arrive in numbers all fancied up in their best. This was turning out to be the event of the year around these parts!

The preacher came and asked to see Samara and Molly escorted him to her room. Alan went to his room and started to dress for the occasion. He had found earlier in the closet a nice shirt, pants and a dress jacket that all fit him very well. He polished hid boots and got dressed. When he came out the preacher met him and told Alan how pretty his future wife was looking. Alan thanked him and walked to the porch.

What a crowd, Alan thought, a lot of people and everyone was coming up to him and congratulated him on his big day. They all thanked him for the chance to be there. Alan thought of what the Old Indian had said to be alert. But with this many people, and half of them carrying guns, how would Mark Hayes be dumb enough to try and start anything here? But then again maybe Mark would plan an ambush. Not likely to happen though as Sam Griffin had place sentries in several prime locations.

The big hour was about to begin. It was five minutes to two and all the gals that could were on the porch to be bridesmaids. The preacher motioned to Alan and Sam, Alan's choice for best man, to take their places. The preacher then motioned to the musicians to get ready and held his hand up. It was so quiet you could here a cat scratch.

The preacher lowed his hand and they all started to play "Here Comes the Bride." Alan's knees were getting a bit shaky and Sam patted him on the shoulder for confidence.

The first out the door was Molly, a bouquet in her hand and a grin from ear to ear. Next was Samara and as she appeared the crowd just wowed, she was so lovely. She held a nice flower arrangement and her eyes were beginning to water, but she was smiling brightly. She was a thing of beauty. Alan felt so warm, happy and so very lucky. The preacher stood before them and said as he looked to the crowd; "Friends we all are gathered here today to witness the joining of these two in the in the bliss of holly matrimony. I will ask now if anyone knows why these two should not be joined together, speak now or forever hold your peace!"

It was silent. The preacher waited for a few seconds and turned back to Alan and Samara.

Suddenly a voice shouted; "I do!" It was Mark Hayes standing there with a Colt in both hands looking mighty angry. There were enough clicks of cocking guns, it sounded like hail on a wooden roof. Marshal Ed Buist was flabbergasted. He thought that Mark was truly insane. Alan and Samara couldn't believe what was taking place.

"That should be my woman, and this my ranch." Mark said. The crowd backed away and left Mark standing there alone. Every available gun was pointing at him, but the chances of an innocent bystander getting hit, was very likely.

"What do you have ta' say now Miss Halleck?" Mark asked.

Samara whispered to Alan; "Let me handle this my own way an' don't try to stop me."

"Samara, what are you gonna' do?" Alan said.

"Let me handle this Alan."
"Mark your right," Samara said, "I should marry you, you'll take care of me. Won't you?"
"Damn right woman, the best there is. Glad you finally got smart an' realized it, and the preacher is here."
The whole crowd was in shock to hear what Samara just said. People were standing there with their mouths and eyes open big. All eyes were on Samara and Mark.
"What are you saying Samara?" Alan asked.
"Just back off Alan. This is my fight now. I know what I'm doing."
"But what you just told Mark. Honey I love you!"
"I love you too Alan, now let me handle this so we can get on with our wedding." Samara looked at Mark: "You want me big boy? Come here and give me a big hug to prove it." With that said, the whole crowd was taken back. Had she lost her mind and her dignity?
Mark came up to Samara with a big grin on his face. He pushed his Colt's back into their holster and grabbed Samara. He towered over her as he wrapped his arms around her. Samara was lost in his arms.
The crowd could not believe what they were witnessing. Suddenly there was a muffled pop like sound. Marks eyes opened wide and his mouth gritted tight as he stepped back blood coming from his stomach. He was dazed, confused.
"That was for my Dad Mark," Samara said holding a two shot derringer, "And this is for me!" She said as she shot him in the forehead. Mark went over backward, dead. Samara threw the pistol to Molly and kissed Alan. The crowd cheered, Ed shook his head in disbelief. Charlie

Lassiter hollered out; "That's Cliff's baby girl. See's just like her Ole Man."
"Thank you Mr. Charlie," Samara said and pointed to Mark's body, "Can someone clear up the yard so we can get along with my wedding?"
The crowd re-gathered and the ceremony went nicely. Molly was in tears and so were most of the gal's. After kissing the bride, Alan and Samara greeted and thank every one as they lined up to give their congratulations. Hunter Hurst asked if he could stay on with his sister Haley and work for the Halleck Ranch. Alan and Samara agreed he could, as he was such a help putting the pieces together. Marshal Ed Buist tipped his hat at Samara, shook Alan's hand and said; "Congratulations you two, I'm so very happy for you both. And also, Mrs. Halleck, in case there are any questions, I stand as a witness that you shot in self defense as he was obviously trying to smother you in front of everyone here." Alan and Samara laughed.
Charlie Lassiter and his son's wished them the best and Charlie said to Alan; "Hope you can hang on son, her father Cliff, told me she was a Spitfire Mustang."
"Oh Mr. Charlie," Samara said, "I was just spoiled rotten by my Dad. Now's it's Alan's turn."
The wedding party was a huge success. The roasted steer was plenty to feed all and folks were told to take some home when they leave. There was dancing, singing and plenty to drink for all. About nine o'clock Samara said; "OK cowboy, lets see if you can handle a mustang," and gave him a serious kiss. They went to the house, locked the door, and blew out the lights.

About Al Hartman

Al Hartman has been a free lance writer for over thirty years. He has written for newspapers, magazines and periodicals. Having been around horses all his life the old west has, and always is, in his mind. Maybe it's because Ernest Hemmingway is a distant cousin, or so they say, and Al has read all of Hemmingway's novels.

Al wanted for years to write about the old west adventures but never found time to sit long enough to do it. He raced motorcycles for Triumph, Yamaha and many others. He and his father had a successful business for nearly forty years. He has been and still is a avid treasure hunter. Loves hunting, fishing and being in the outdoors. Finally one day he came up with an idea of writing a story about a Texas to Missouri cattle drive in 1893. It was called, "The Last Drive." When asked by some after they read his book; "How did you come up with all this action?" Al replied; "All I had to work with was the beginning and the end, a cattle drive from Texas to Missouri, the rest I had to make up." The Last Drive took a year to write with a lot of research and planning the next moves as the story went on. It is listed as, "Historical Fiction."

Al's next book was a follow up to The Last Drive, called "Texas Bound." "Spitfire Mustang" takes place in 1876 and a lot of the characters in this book are shown as what they did in earlier years. Al is now writing a short story book that will be released shortly called "To Tame the West." When asked, Al said; "I wish I had started writing westerns earlier."

Made in the USA
San Bernardino, CA
24 November 2015